Would You Rather…

by

Kimberly Baer

The Haunting of Pinedale High

Would You Rather…

Contact Information: info@thewildrosepress.com

Cover Art by *The Wild Rose Press, Inc.*

The Wild Rose Press, Inc.
PO Box 708
Adams Basin, NY 14410-0708
Visit us at www.thewildrosepress.com

Publishing History
First Edition, 2025
Trade Paperback ISBN 978-1-5092-6014-0
Digital ISBN 978-1-5092-6015-7

The Haunting of Pinedale High
Published in the United States of America

Dedication

For Koa and Khloe, whose love affair with books is just beginning.

Chapter 1

Henry

"Ma, come on. You gotta let me go to school today."

"Out of the question, Henry. You have strep throat."

"You don't know that. Not yet, anyway. When is the doctor's office going to call with the test results?"

"I don't know. Soon, I hope."

"If the test is negative, can I go to school?"

"No! You have a fever. The school nurse would send you right back home."

"Not if she doesn't know about the fever. *I'm* not going to tell her."

"You're probably contagious. Do you want to make your classmates sick?"

"I'll keep away from everybody, I promise. Please, can I go to school?"

"No."

"There's a cross-country meet today. The team's counting on me."

"You can't run cross country with a fever."

"Sure I can. I feel fine."

"Well, you're not fine."

"Please, Ma. Please. If you let me go, I'll wash your car after school. How about that? I'll even make dinner."

"Oh, for God's sake. How did I end up with a kid like you? When I was a girl, I tried every trick in the book to get out of going to school. But you? You'd show up on the weekends if they let you. You'd go on Christmas Day."

"What can I say? I love school. I don't want to miss out on anything."

"It's a random Monday in September. What could you possibly miss out on?"

"You never know, Ma. You never know."

Chapter 2

Blake

The substitute teacher looked like a mythical creature—in Blake Pedley's humble opinion, anyway. The guy could have passed for a gnome or a leprechaun or a troll, or maybe a hobbit. Blake wasn't positive about *hobbit* because he hadn't seen those movies. His friend Ava had, though. Multiple times. Blake craned his head to the left, trying to catch her eye. Hoping to make her smile when he jerked his head toward the sub and mouthed the word *hobbit*. But Ava wouldn't look over. She was doodling on the cover of her physics notebook as she waited for class to begin.

The sub was short and stocky with overlarge ears and a close-cropped brown beard. Big feet, too. He stood at the whiteboard with his elbows bent and his fists clenched, like he was getting ready to punch somebody.

"Good morning, class. I'm Mr. Trinkley, and I'll be filling in for Mr. Zwick today." The guy's icy blue gaze swept across the room, taking everybody in. Trying to suss out the troublemakers, thought Blake. Twenty-three pairs of eyes stared back. Ordinarily, there would have been twenty-four, but Henry Schiffhauer was absent today.

Laughter erupted in the classroom across the hall.

Mr. Trinkley strode over to close the door, and for some reason, that simple act reminded Blake of someone sealing a submarine hatch before the vessel sank down, down, down into the ocean.

Mr. Trinkley paced in front of Mr. Zwick's desk. "As you probably know, substitute teachers aren't experts in any particular subject area. I'm no exception. I am not a physics teacher. I am essentially a babysitter. My job is to take attendance and provide supervision, nothing more. So the question is—" He stopped pacing and turned to face the class. "—how are we going to spend the next forty-five minutes?"

Blake wasn't sure if that was a rhetorical question, so he didn't say anything. But some of his classmates called out suggestions.

"Study hall!"

"Nap time!"

"Phone time!"

"Par-tay!" That one came from Blake's friend Deej, whose actual name was Duncan Nolty Junior. Deej flipped his sandy-blond bangs out of his eyes and flashed a devilish grin around the room. Blake noticed that his gaze lingered longest on Maddy Eppley.

Brianna McFeaters said primly, "I think we should spend this time reading the next chapter in our textbook. That's what Mr. Zwick would want."

Jared Crofton booed her.

Mr. Trinkley said, "That's a fine idea, Miss McFeaters, and one I'll consider. I have an idea of my own, so let me put this to the class. Would you rather spend the period reading your physics textbook? Or—" His eyes glimmered with a strange light. "—would you like to play a game?"

4

"Game! Game!" The chant started immediately, and within a few seconds, the whole class had taken it up. All except for Brianna, who scowled and slunk down in her seat, clearly miffed to have had her idea rejected.

Mr. Trinkley reached into a scuffed leather satchel on Mr. Zwick's desk and pulled out a small tray and a stack of cards. He did some fancy shuffling, like a Vegas poker dealer, and fanned the cards across the tray, face down.

"The game is called 'Would you rather.' Printed on each card is a scenario that presents two options. You will each draw a card and read it aloud. You'll then make your choice and explain your reasoning. Others may weigh in on the pros and cons of each alternative."

DeShawn Yancy raised his hand. "How is that a game? Like, what's the point?"

"The point is seeing how your minds work. Trust me, it'll be fun."

When Mr. Trinkley smiled, Blake saw that his canines were longer and pointier than his other teeth, giving him the look of a wolf. Blake had a neighbor with teeth like that. The neighborhood kids called him Wolfgang.

Mr. Trinkley walked over to Alyssa Aiken—first row, first seat—and held out the tray of cards. "You're up, Miss Aiken. Pick a card, any card."

Alyssa chose the first card on the pile and read aloud, " 'Would you rather be an amazing artist or a brilliant mathematician?' " She didn't even pause to think about it. "Amazing artist."

Mr. Trinkley gave a short laugh that might have been edged with scorn. "That was fast. Give us your rationale. Why did you choose artist?"

"Because math is stupid."

Mr. Trinkley turned to face the rest of the class. "Anyone disagree?"

Blake's friend Charlie Washington spoke up. "Math is not stupid! My cousin's good at math, and she got a scholarship because of it."

"Artistic people get scholarships, too," Valentina Sanchez pointed out.

Others chimed in. Math was more useful. Beautiful art made people happy. Math smarts could land you a good job—accountant, statistician, financial analyst. But art could be a job, too, or a hobby, or both. Through it all, Alyssa twirled a strand of purple hair around her forefinger, her blue eyes vacant. Blake wasn't sure she was even listening.

After the discussion died down, Mr. Trinkley turned to Alyssa. "What's your final answer?"

Alyssa untwirled her hair and folded her hands on her desk. "I'm sticking with artist."

The art enthusiasts in the room woo-hooed. The math advocates rolled their eyes.

Paisley Boyd drew the next card. " 'Would you rather have swollen hands or swollen feet?' " She laughed uncertainly. "That's a weird one. I guess I'll go with feet? I do a lot of texting. I can't afford to be fat-fingering my phone."

No one disagreed.

Then it was Jared Crofton's turn. " 'Would you rather win a thousand dollars or be honored for doing something heroic?' " Jared grinned. "Sweet! What did I do that was so heroic?"

"That's unknown," said Mr. Trinkley. "The only

information we have is what's on the card."

"I'll take the thousand bucks," said Jared. "Been wanting to pimp out my car."

"Money over fame. Interesting," said Mr. Trinkley.

He moved on to Maddy Eppley, who drew a card from the middle of the pile. Maddy's big brown eyes got even bigger as they swept across the card, giving her the look of a spooked cat. She glanced up at Mr. Trinkley. "Can I pick a different card instead?"

"No. What you get is what you get. Read the card to the class, Miss Eppley."

Maddy's voice trembled as she read. " 'Would you rather accidentally kill someone or be kidnapped by a serial killer?' "

"Holy crap," murmured Kylie Wentworth.

"Um, neither." Maddy tried to put the card back on the tray, but Mr. Trinkley blocked her hand.

"Not an option. You must choose one of the given alternatives."

Deej said, "But they both suck!"

"The cards mirror real life," said Mr. Trinkley, responding to Deej but looking at Maddy. "That's one of the points of this game. Sometimes, there's no good option, and all you can do is choose what you consider to be the lesser of the evils."

Maddy hunched over her desk, staring at the card. Her brown hair hung down the sides of her face, leaving only the small bump of her nose visible.

Charlie said, "I'd go with the first option. If you kill somebody by accident, you won't go to jail."

"I don't want to kill somebody at all! But—" Maddy tossed her head in anguish. "—I don't want to get murdered by a serial killer either."

"The card doesn't say anything about getting murdered," said Zoe Malinowski. "It just says kidnapped. You might get rescued."

"Might," said Charlie.

Maddy looked at the card again. "It's too hard. I can't decide."

Reina Ichikawa, who sat behind Maddy, patted her on the shoulder. "It's okay, Mads. This isn't real. It's just a silly game."

"Yeah, okay. I guess—I guess I'll pick serial killer and hope for the best." She glanced around the room and caught Blake's eye. "I can't kill somebody. I just can't."

Blake wasn't sure which of the two options he would have chosen. He was glad that card was gone.

Of course, there might be worse ones in the pile.

The mood of the room had shifted in a way that troubled him. That game-day euphoria was gone. People were shooting uneasy glances at one another.

Mr. Trinkley moved on to Reina, who had to choose between going bald and growing excessive body hair. She decided going bald would be preferable. "I'd rather die than be hairy!"

"A moot point," said Mr. Trinkley, "since death is not one of the options on the card."

Then it was Deej's turn. Deej was Blake's neighbor and one of his closest friends. He was also the junior class jokester. Blake suspected he used humor to compensate for his crappy home life.

Deej stared at his card for a long time. Then he shot Mr. Trinkley a dark look. "This is effed up."

Mr. Trinkley said, "Read the card aloud, Mr. Nolty."

8

Deej's mouth twisted like he was chewing something nasty. He read, " 'Would you rather die of cancer or be killed in a vehicular collision?' "

A horrified silence followed. Jared mumbled, "That's harsh."

Deej said flatly, "So either way, I'm screwed."

"Some may see it that way," said Mr. Trinkley. "Regardless, you must choose. Surely one scenario is preferable to the other."

Deej shook his head, his lips pressed together. Mr. Trinkley glanced around the classroom. "Thoughts, anyone?"

For the longest time, no one spoke. Finally, Charlie said, "If you die fast, you don't suffer. Dying slow gives you time to reflect back on your life."

"That's one way to look at it," said Mr. Trinkley.

"Fine," said Deej. "Then kill me in an accident. I've only lived for sixteen years. I don't have much to reflect back on."

Blake wondered if everyone else was as eager for class to end as he was. He glanced at the clock. Twenty-five minutes to go. He wished the bell would ring before his turn came up, but that was unlikely. There were only six people between him and *would you rather.*

His heart thudded sickly, a fight-or-flight response with no rational basis. He drew in a deep breath and let it out slowly, trying to calm himself. *Everything is fine. It's just a silly game.*

But was it? His gut insisted something was very wrong.

Mr. Trinkley moved to the next desk and then the next. Blake felt like a fly caught in a web, waiting for the spider to scuttle over and devour him. *Would you rather s*cenarios flowed into his ears and took root in his imagination, like horror-movie shorts.

Would you rather live in a house infested by bedbugs or by spiders?

Would you rather roast to death or freeze to death?

Would you rather have a grotesque rash or chronic diarrhea?

The room blurred and shimmied around him, and he clutched the edges of his desk to steady himself. This whole situation seemed surreal, like a dream. A nightmare, actually. Why were so many of the scenarios bad? Nobody'd had a good one since Jared.

A shape materialized at Blake's side, dark as a shadow. "Your turn, Mr. Pedley."

Blake wondered suddenly how Mr. Trinkley knew everybody's name. Had he memorized the seating chart before class started? That didn't seem possible unless the guy had a photographic memory.

Blake eyed the tray apprehensively. The cards were no longer lined up neatly but had gotten jumbled, like objects jostled around by an earthquake. The card backs were ivory in color, though it was possible they'd started out bright white and had yellowed over the course of many years. Each one featured a dark blue star with a staring eye in the middle of it. A fancy curlicue design danced around the border.

Blake reached for a card near the middle of the pile but then withdrew his hand. He almost chose a card that was half hidden under several others but changed his mind. He finally selected a card that was off by itself in a corner of the tray.

He winced as he turned it over. He read aloud,

" 'Would you rather lose a limb or be without a cell phone for the rest of your life?' "

He exhaled slowly as the tension melted out of his shoulders. That one was bad, but not horrendous. At least nobody died.

Blake's classmates were already discussing the scenario. He was surprised by how many people thought it would be better to lose a limb. Kylie said getting a bionic arm might be an option. Liam Oswalt said he would agree to lose a limb if he could choose which limb. Mr. Trinkley said only the fates could decide that.

Blake ultimately chose to be without his cell phone. "I'm kind of attached to my limbs. In more ways than one," he added, recognizing his unintentional play on words. He gave a shaky smile, but Mr. Trinkley didn't smile back. No one did.

When Mr. Trinkley moved on to the next person, Blake reached down to squeeze the front pocket of his backpack. Thank God. His phone was still there.

Chapter 3

Mrs. Hendrickson

School secretary Nancy Hendrickson had never seen Principal Kouriki so angry. "Fix it, Nancy. Fix it now. But first, email all the homeroom teachers and tell them to collect the student handbooks." She paced in a tight circle in front of Nancy's desk. "Not that it'll work. The students won't want to give them back, especially if they know about *this*. They'll claim they lost their book, and how can we prove otherwise?" She gave Nancy a scathing look. "This is a disaster."

She went into her office and slammed the door.

Nancy sighed wearily. The second week of school was off to a rip-roaring start. As one of the two office secretaries, she was busy all day every day, with an hour for lunch to decompress. Now she had a mess to deal with in addition to juggling her regular duties.

The calamity had unfolded earlier this morning, when a parent had called Principal Kouriki to complain about a typo in the student handbook. A rather egregious typo, actually—the word "pubic" used in place of "public." The error might not have been so bad if it had been buried in a dense block of text, but that wasn't the case. It was in a bolded heading in size fourteen font: *Pubic Displays of Affection.* Damn that idiot intern who'd worked in the office over the summer. Someone should have checked her work more carefully. Nancy herself should have checked. But the girl was a college senior, an English major. Nancy had expected better from her.

Nancy made the correction on her computer and then scrolled back to the beginning of the document. Might as well comb through the whole thing to make sure there were no other errors. That would take at least an hour. Then she would have to call the printing company to see how quickly they could reprint the books. Meanwhile, there were emails to be answered and several meetings to set up.

"Excuse me? Ma'am?"

Nancy's nerves jangled as she turned toward the front of the office. A young man stood at the counter, wearing a dress shirt and a tie. He looked like a kid fresh out of college, all bright-eyed and rosy-cheeked, full of optimism about the future. He'd better hope he never ended up working in a school office, Nancy thought sourly. That guileless good cheer would be squashed like a bug under a principal's high-heeled pump.

Nancy sauntered over to the counter and forced herself to smile. "May I help you?"

"I'm sorry I'm late. I'm Mr. Volk? I'm supposed to fill in for Mr. Zwick today."

Nancy stared at him in confusion. "You're the substitute? But we already have a sub for Mr. Zwick's classes."

The sub had arrived in the midst of the *pubic* commotion. Nancy had gotten a brief impression of a short guy with a beard and cool blue eyes. The bell for first period was about to ring, so she'd skipped the usual formalities and sent him directly to room 113. She'd told him to stop by the office later to take care of the admin stuff. In her haste to get him to Mr. Zwick's classroom, she hadn't even asked his name.

"I'm pretty sure I'm supposed to be the sub," Mr. Volk said firmly. "Someone called me last night to set it up."

"Right. That would have been me." Nancy was the point person for teacher absences. Her husband griped every time her job encroached on her home life, but that was what she'd agreed to when she'd taken the job. "You said your name is Volk? Yes, I do remember calling you."

The question was, who had called the other guy? Maybe June, the assistant principal's secretary, though that seemed unlikely. Lining up subs wasn't her job, and June wasn't the type to go above and beyond. Nancy craned her head toward June's desk, but June was missing. Probably off gossiping with the school librarian.

Maybe Mr. Zwick himself had called the other sub, thought Nancy, though that seemed equally unlikely. Besides, he would have mentioned it when he'd called last night to report his upcoming absence.

Well, wasn't this peachy. Nancy hoped the school wouldn't have to pay both subs. She was in enough trouble with Principal Kouriki.

The bell rang, signaling the end of first period. "Come with me," said Nancy, marching around the side of the counter.

She felt like a salmon swimming upstream as she led Mr. Volk up the crowded hallway to Mr. Zwick's classroom. The room was empty. The students who'd been there during first period were on their way to their next class. But where was the bearded guy?

"This is where you're supposed to be," she told Mr. Volk. "When the other guy shows up, send him down to the office. We'll get this sorted out."

But the first sub never showed up, and Nancy soon forgot he'd been there in the first place. She had enough to worry about with *pubic*.

Chapter 4

Ava

"Ava! Ava, wait up."

Ava heard Blake calling but didn't slow her pace. She couldn't. She was on the verge of hurling and hoped to do it in a toilet rather than all over people's shoes in the middle of the crowded hallway. The girls' restroom was up ahead. Ava pumped her legs faster, her fine blonde hair streaming behind her, but just before she reached the door, somebody grabbed her arm, stopping her in her tracks.

"Ava! Hey."

Blake had caught up with her.

Ava sucked in a deep breath, a trick she'd used in the past to temporarily soothe a roiling stomach. But she kept a foot pointed toward the girls' room door in case she had to dash for a toilet.

"Are you okay?" asked Blake. His hazel eyes were soft with concern. "That game was pretty intense."

Ava nodded, not daring to open her mouth. Blake was a good friend and a nice guy, but she didn't think he would appreciate having vomit spewed all over him.

"That guy was creepy," Blake said. "I don't think he's ever subbed here before. I've never seen him before, anyway." He shook his head ruefully. "It sucks that you got such crappy options. I could tell you were

16

freaked out. Just be glad it wasn't real."

Blake was right, of course—it wasn't real. But back in class, when she'd drawn that terrible card, it had seemed real. A feeling of impending doom had spread through her, as if whatever choice she made would become her destiny. Now, though, the horror was receding. The nausea, too. All around her, people laughed and chattered as they headed to their next class. Somewhere beyond the brick walls, the sun was shining. The idea of having your fate determined by words on a card suddenly seemed absurd, a plot from a bad movie.

She managed a weak smile. "Yeah. That was crazy."

Two people stepped out of the flow of traffic to join them. Charlie and Deej.

"Yo, Quartet," said Charlie, with a circular wave of his hand.

Deej locked eyes with Ava. "You and me, A. We sure can pick 'em."

Ava gave a doleful eye roll. "Won't argue with that, D."

Ava, Blake, Charlie, and Deej. Same age, lifelong neighbors, best buds since nursery school. They'd been seven when Deej had dubbed them the Alphabet Quartet. The name hadn't caught on among their schoolmates, but they'd gotten a kick out of calling themselves that. Still did. It wasn't every foursome that had first names starting with consecutive letters of the alphabet.

"So, what do you guys think I should wear to my funeral?" asked Deej.

"How about that tux from your cousin's wedding?"

suggested Charlie. "You looked mighty snatched in that."

"Dude, that was rented. Anyway, it might not matter. I'll probably have a closed casket. You know, because of the car accident. I might be pretty banged up."

"A closed casket would be better, actually," said Charlie. "Nobody wants to stand around looking at your ugly face."

Charlie could afford to joke. Of the four of them, he was the only one who'd picked a card with two positive options: *Would you rather get the romantic partner of your dreams or land the perfect job?* Charlie had chosen the job, which hadn't surprised Ava. Charlie was smart and practical. He was also a good-looking Black kid who had no trouble attracting girls. Card or no card, his future was bound to include both the perfect job and the wife of his dreams.

Charlie turned to Ava. "How you doing, A? Your card sucked pretty bad, too."

"I have to go," Ava said. She turned abruptly and headed down the hall. Too bad if her friends thought she was rude. She couldn't stand to listen to another word about *would you rather.* She hoped everyone would be done talking about it the next time the quartet got together.

She shuddered as she thought back on the game. She'd sensed from the beginning that something was wrong. Clammy hands and a racing heart didn't lie. She felt as if she'd stepped into an alternate universe where dark magic ruled. Others had felt it, too. She'd seen the fear on their faces as they'd drawn their cards.

When it was Ava's turn, she'd folded her arms

across her rib cage and said, "I'm not playing."

Up close, Mr. Trinkley's eyes looked steely, more gray than blue. Or maybe they changed color according to his mood. He said, "Everyone is playing, Miss Wilkinson."

Ava's father always told her to stand up for her convictions, so she said, more forcefully, "I don't like this game, and I don't want to play."

"I see," said Mr. Trinkley. He made a *tsk-tsk* sound. "So you're a quitter."

Ava tilted her chin higher. "I'm not a quitter. I just don't want to play this particular game."

"Fine," said Mr. Trinkley. "Don't play. But I think Mr. Zwick will be interested to hear about your uncooperativeness."

Ava gaped at him. She hadn't expected that. And, oh, it wasn't fair! She wasn't being uncooperative. She was merely asking to be excused from an activity that made her uncomfortable.

Ava couldn't afford to get in trouble with Mr. Zwick. The guy already had it out for her, and this would only make matters worse. As crazy as it sounded, Mr. Zwick seemed to resent her for being a good student. He was a newish teacher, possibly a little insecure. He constantly belittled her, making her feel like she was being a cocky know-it-all. She wasn't, though. She just happened to be good at physics. What was she supposed to do, play dumb?

She squeezed her eyes shut, trying to overcome the cognitive dissonance that swirled in her head. It occurred to her that she was already playing *would you rather*, and this scenario was as unwinnable as some of the others she'd heard. *Would you rather play a scary game or get in trouble with Mr. Zwick?*

Mr. Trinkley had turned his back on her. He was moving on to the next student.

"Wait," said Ava. "Okay. I'll play."

Mr. Trinkley turned around. When he smiled, his eyes glittered like moonlit ice. Something told Ava he'd known she would give in.

Her hand shook as it hovered over the pile of cards. Three times she reached for a card. Three times she pulled her hand away. Finally, she took the very last card in the pile. Her throat seized up as she read the words on it. Oh God. This was worse than she'd imagined.

She stared at the card for so long that Mr. Trinkley had to prompt her. "Read the card aloud, Miss Wilkinson."

Ava tried to speak, but her voice kept fracturing. "Would you rather—would you ra—would—" She gulped and blurted it out. " 'Would you rather go missing forever or have the person you love most go missing forever?' "

Chapter 5

Blake

Reina Ichikawa had the most gorgeous hair—thick, black, and glossy. Blake sat behind her in English class, and sometimes, it was all he could do not to reach out and run his fingers through it. He imagined how it would feel—cool and silky, like a waterfall. He wondered if thoughts like that made him a creeper. Did he have an Asian hair fetish? No, he was pretty sure he was just envious. Blake's own hair was a nondescript Caucasian brown, coarse rather than thick. He couldn't coax a shine out of it, no matter how much conditioner he applied.

Blake continued to study Reina's head as Mrs. Pelegrino diagrammed a sentence on the whiteboard. Reina's center part was perfectly straight, like a coastal highway, and there was a small, round patch of bare scalp where the part ended at the back of her head. That bald spot reminded Blake of the circular area at the end of a cul-de-sac where you could turn your car around without having to back up.

That bald spot. Blake frowned, his eyes fixed on it. Something niggled at him, a message from his subconscious that he couldn't quite read… Wait, he had it. A few days ago, Reina's bald spot had been dime-sized. Today, it was nickel-sized. And a week or two ago, it hadn't been there at all. Blake was sure about that. He knew Reina's head better than he knew his own because he stared at it so often.

Was Reina losing her hair? Blake's breath caught in his throat as he thought back on that day in physics class when the sub had made them play that weird game. That had been two weeks ago, and he'd barely thought of it since then. He'd pushed the whole thing out of his mind because the feelings it stirred up in him were so unpleasant. But now the memories rushed back, including the scenario on Reina's card: *Would you rather go bald or grow excessive body hair?* Reina had chosen the going-bald option.

Was Reina's choice coming true?

Blake stifled a laugh. He was being ridiculous. *Fanciful,* his grandma would have said. Lots of girls probably had cul-de-sac circles on their heads. He'd just never noticed before.

Nonetheless, he reached down and groped the front of his backpack until his fingers found the sturdy rectangle of his cell phone.

Still there.

Chapter 6

Alyssa

Alyssa Aiken twirled her mechanical pencil like a mini baton as she glowered down at the blank sheet of notebook paper on her bedroom desk. Homework sucked, and math homework was the worst of all. Why had quadratic equations even been invented? Did anybody use them in real life?

Alyssa hated math—always had, always would. She didn't get why she had to take it, considering that her dream was to be a hair stylist and someday own her own hair salon. She didn't think you needed much math for that. But the state of North Carolina required four math credits to graduate, so here she was, wading through math three.

Her thoughts drifted back to the dumb game that creepy sub had made them play in physics class. *Which would you choose* or some such thing. Alyssa's card had offered a choice between being a brilliant mathematician and an amazing artist. She'd chosen artist because of her aversion to math. Why would she want to be good at something she would never use again once her education was complete?

She laid her pencil down and leaned back in her chair. Wouldn't it be great if she really was an amazing artist? That would open up some new career possibilities. Instead of becoming a hair stylist, maybe she could be a graphic designer or a children's book illustrator. Better yet, she might not have to get a job at all. She could stay home and churn out magnificent paintings, which she would then sell for thousands of dollars apiece.

Too bad she sucked at art as bad as she sucked at math.

But did she, though? She hadn't tried anything remotely artsy since seventh grade, the last time she'd taken an art class. She was older now, more focused and less flighty. Maybe art would come easier. Maybe she should give it another try.

Maybe she should give it a try right now.

What to draw, that was the question. Alyssa glanced around the room. Her eyes landed on a framed photograph on her dresser, a memory of a fun day at an amusement park with her friends Amber and Stef. Alyssa set the photo on her desk and positioned her pencil over the notebook paper that should have been covered in quadratic equations by now.

And then something magical happened. Alyssa's right hand started moving, and it seemed to know exactly what to do. Rounded blobs morphed into heads with recognizable faces. She captured Amber's exuberant grin, Stef's snarky smirk. Her own practiced smile. Sunlight glinted off the tops of their heads and made logical shadows beneath their noses. A twisty rollercoaster track loomed in the background, its framework rendered in intricate detail. The sketching process took less than fifteen minutes, and when she was done, Alyssa could only stare in wonder.

Holy crap. She really was an amazing artist.

Chapter 7

Ava

Of the four people in the Alphabet Quartet, Ava was the one with the best home life. She knew it, and so did the others, though they'd never discussed it.

Deej's dad was a functioning alcoholic, and that was as good as it got, because the dad was essentially his only parent. Eight years ago Deej's mom had moved to California with her lover—some older guy, a real estate mogul—and Deej rarely heard from her. Ava hated going to Deej's house because the place was always a mess and smelled like a mix of scorched onions and dirty feet. The lack of feminine influence was apparent, and if that way of thinking made her sexist—fine. She would own it.

Blake and his younger brother, Max, also lived in a single-parent household. Their dad had been killed in a military accident when Blake was four. Mrs. Pedley was a loving parent who made a good living as a nurse practitioner, but there was only so much a single mom could do for two boys.

Charlie's family was intact, and his parents were perfectly nice people, but they owned a hardware store and were so busy managing it that they didn't have much time for Charlie and his three younger sisters. Charlie was frequently called upon to babysit.

Then there were Ava's parents—fully present, non-alcoholic, utterly devoted to Ava and her brother, Jordan. Ava loved them with all her heart, though if pressed she would have had to admit that she loved her father a smidgeon more. Likewise, she sensed that her dad loved her a tiny bit more than he loved her brother. The two of them had a special bond, and that was okay because Ava's mother and Jordan had their own special bond.

Ava's dad was the only one in the family with a hint of a southern twang, just enough to make him sound folksy and affable. When Ava was little, she'd loved hearing him read bedtime stories, because he made all the characters sound so friendly, even the grumpy ones.

Her dad was the one she wanted at her bedside when she was sick. He was the first person she thought of when she had a success to share, an A-plus test or an award certificate. Ava's dad was the person she loved best in all the world, and there was no way she would ever, ever choose to have him go missing, not even in a made-up scenario.

So when she'd drawn that terrible *would you rather* card, she'd chosen to have herself go missing instead.

The problem was, if she ever did go missing, it would destroy her dad. So maybe her choice had been a selfish one after all.

A cool evening breeze wafted across Ava's face as she slapped her history book shut. She sat on the front porch swing, toeing herself gently back and forth. She'd come out here to study for a quiz but was having trouble concentrating. Her mind kept snapping back to that awful day in physics class, even though seven weeks had passed since then. *Would you rather* hadn't really been a game, just a sadist's attempt to freak out a bunch of teenagers. *None of the scenarios were going to come true.* She kept telling herself that, but part of her refused to buy it. She still remembered how freaked out she'd felt, for no reason she could articulate.

Something thumped in her chest, a rhythmic boom, boom, boom. At first she thought she was having heart palpitations. Then she realized she was feeling the amplified bass of a car stereo. Ava put her hands over her ears as the noise got louder. She watched a car come into view and was surprised to see that it was Jared Crofton's car. Jared lived two blocks up the street. He drove a modest compact car, but he'd obviously made some upgrades. Tinted windows, a spoiler on the back, new tires, and—impossible to ignore—a more powerful stereo system. Jared would be lucky if he made it to twenty without going deaf.

After Jared's car cruised by, Ava opened her history book, determined to try again. And shut it just as quickly. Hadn't Jared's *would you rather* card said something about winning a thousand bucks? And hadn't Jared said he would use the money to pimp out his car?

Chapter 8

Blake

"It's super weird," said Ava, leaning against the locker next to Blake's. "You can't deny that."

"It's weird all right," said Blake. "How did Jared manage to buy a lottery ticket when he isn't even eighteen?"

Ava shook her head impatiently. "*He* didn't buy it. His uncle did. And cashed it in for him when he won. But that's not the important thing."

Blake twisted his combination lock right, then left, then right, and swung his locker door open. He wished Ava would go away. He didn't feel like discussing *would you rather*, not today, anyway. He had concerns of his own but wasn't ready to share them with her. She tended to freak out every time the subject came up.

"That day," Ava pressed on, "Jared picked the option of winning a thousand bucks. And a few weeks later, what happens? He wins a thousand bucks."

Blake shoved his history book into his locker and pulled out his French book. "I'll admit it's a weird coincidence. But coincidences happen. Like that time my brother broke my mom's favorite vase, and then we saw one exactly like it in the thrift store window."

Ava flipped her blonde hair over her shoulders. "I'm not sure I believe in coincidences. In Jared's case,

I definitely don't."

"Ava! It's been almost two months. None of the other things have come true. I still have my cell phone. Deej is alive and well." Blake spoke more sharply than he'd intended.

"Oh, nice. So we should wait for Deej to die before we do something?"

"What could we do? If that dude put a curse on us, we're all screwed."

"Yeah. But some worse than others." She threw him a bitter look. "You lose your cell phone. I disappear forever. Thanks for the support, friend."

She flounced off down the hall.

Blake slammed his locker shut. Great. Now Ava was mad at him. He decided to let her cool off and then smooth things over with her after school. She usually didn't stay mad for too long.

As he walked to French class, he spotted Reina up ahead, moving books around in her locker. Blake's heart gave a little lurch. He was still assessing the hair situation and was more perplexed than ever. Not just perplexed. Uneasy, too.

Shortly after he'd noticed Reina's bald spot, she'd changed her hairstyle. She'd done away with the part and had instead taken to brushing her hair straight back from her forehead and securing it into a ponytail at the nape of her neck. That made Blake think she knew about the bald spot and was trying to cover it up.

But then, a week ago, she'd started wearing her hair loose again. The center part was back, and the bald spot was gone. Had she been applying a special ointment that accelerated hair growth? Had she gotten a hair transplant? Was she wearing a wig?

Blake pondered the situation and decided *wig* was the most plausible explanation. The color of Reina's hair seemed subtly different, a matte sooty-black instead of its usual shimmery blue-black. If she was, in fact, wearing a wig, it was probably because her bald spot had gotten bigger, which would mean her curse was coming true. And if that was the case, Blake wanted to know about it.

He felt an overpowering urge to touch Reina's hair. He had never done that before, but his eyes had. His eyes knew its bulk, its texture, and he felt that his fingers had somehow absorbed that same knowledge. Would a wig feel different from Reina's natural hair? He thought it would. A few seconds with his fingers in her hair, and he would know the truth.

He and Reina weren't exactly best buds, but they were on amicable terms. Sometimes, they chatted before English class started. Reina liked to talk about her favorite TV show, an angsty teen drama that Blake didn't watch. Lately, though, she hadn't been very talkative.

He made a hasty plan—a light, playful tug and then: *Hey, Reina, how do you think you did on that grammar quiz?* Nothing creepy about that.

Reina's back was to Blake. His heart pounded as he approached her. He reached out. His hand closed around a thick hank of hair—

—and at that precise moment, Reina dropped into a squat to fetch something from the bottom of her locker. Blake was left holding her hair.

He gaped at the thing dangling from his hand like a dead, boneless critter. *No, no—*

Reina gasped and got to her feet. Her eyes widened

as she saw Blake standing there with her wig in his hand. Blake stared back, his chagrin too big for words. Belatedly, he registered the state of Reina's head. Her beautiful hair had been chopped off to maybe half an inch all around, like a military haircut. She had more bald spots than he could count, giving her head the look of a black dog with white spots. The size of the bald spots varied. The biggest ones were as large and round as half-dollars.

"You idiot!" Reina screeched, her eyes filling with tears. "What is wrong with you?"

The activity in the hallway stilled. People gawked. Reina snatched the wig out of Blake's hand and ran to the girls' restroom.

Nice going, Blake told himself as he slunk up the hall to French class. In the course of a single morning, he'd managed to piss off two girls.

Chapter 9

Maddy

It started raining as Maddy reached the outskirts of town. Too bad she'd forgotten her umbrella. Or, more accurately, opted not to take it. The sky had been somewhat overcast when she'd left the house but hadn't really looked threatening. Now, though, dark clouds roiled overhead, and more were sailing in from the west.

It wasn't raining hard, just sprinkling, but she was getting wetter with each step. She supposed she could go back home to fetch an umbrella, but why bother? Home was a quarter of a mile behind her, whereas her destination was a mere two blocks away. Might as well keep walking. If it was still raining when the meeting was over, one of the kids with a car could drive her home.

She was still hazy about the purpose for the meeting but was going anyway, more out of curiosity than anything. And also because she didn't like to let people down. Blake Pedley had swung by her locker at the end of the day to invite her. "A bunch of us from first-period physics class are meeting in the library community room at six to discuss the sitch. I hope you can make it."

He'd rushed away before Maddy could ask what

sitch he was talking about.

She'd caught Charlie Washington as he trotted to the gym for basketball practice. "Charlie, hey. Blake invited me to a meeting at the library tonight. What's going on?"

"Yeah, it's about that game. Apparently, some people are freaking out. Gotta run, see you there."

That game. Well, that was helpful—not! Did Charlie mean a sports game? If so, which sport? Which game? Football season was over, and basketball season hadn't officially started, though the team held practices several times a week. But wait. Blake had said something about first-period physics class. Could the meeting be about the game that weird sub had made them play a month or two ago?

A shiver went through Maddy as she thought back on that day. She'd had the creepiest feeling the whole time the game was in progress. As if all those chosen fates were destined to come true. Hers had been especially horrific: *get kidnapped by a serial killer.* But as soon as she'd walked out of that classroom, the creepy feeling had evaporated. She'd barely given it a thought since then. This was small, boring Pinedale. What self-respecting serial killer would show up here?

A car rolled up the quiet street, its headlights temporarily blinding her. It stopped when it reached her, and the driver's window went down. Inside was a brown-haired guy with a face that was pleasant, though not really good-looking. Maddy guessed he was in his early thirties. She knew pretty much everybody in town, at least by sight, but she didn't recognize this guy.

"Maddy? Is that you? Wow, you're getting soaked. Can I give you a ride?"

"Um…" She squinted, trying to see him better in the gloom. "Do I know you?"

He grinned. "Sorry! I'm Tommy. I work with Laura. Your mom. I'm one of the new kitchen workers. Your mom introduced us last week when you stopped by the diner after school, remember?"

"Oh, right," Maddy said, though in truth she didn't remember. She felt a stab of shame. How shallow *was* she? If this guy had been hot, she definitely would have remembered him.

Maddy's mom was a server at Lou's Diner, the most popular eatery in town. Maddy often popped in after school to say hi and tell her mom about her day. She and her friends sometimes hung out there in the evenings, too. Lots of kids from school did.

Maddy didn't know the kitchen staff that well, but the servers were like family. Petite, bustling Lacey and tall, giggling Penny and gregarious Mike, who always called her Laura Junior because she looked so much like her mom. Lacey argued that they seemed more like sisters, and Maddy could totally see that. Laura had been barely twenty when Maddy was born.

"So can I give you a ride?" Tommy, the kitchen worker, asked.

Maddy stepped closer to the car. The guy was starting to look familiar. Yeah, she'd definitely seen him around. Still, everything she'd ever learned about stranger danger cycled through her head.

"That's really nice of you. But the library is just up ahead. I won't get much wetter if I walk the rest of the way. It isn't even raining that hard."

Right on cue, the rain poured down harder.

"Uh-oh," said Tommy. "Better hop in, Maddy

Mae."

Maddy Mae. Only her mom called her that.

A giant raindrop splattered on her nose, making her blink.

"I don't want to make you late for—whatever," she said, stalling because she needed just another minute to think.

"You're not making me late for anything. My day is done. I'm heading home to spend a quiet evening with my wife."

His wife. He had a wife. And a home. Maddy pictured a little white house with blue shutters and a flower garden out front.

"You're going in the wrong direction," she said.

"It just so happens I know how to turn around. Learned it in driving school."

He gave her a wink and a smile. He was definitely better looking when he smiled, almost handsome. And *Tommy* was such a friendly name. Maddy smiled back and shucked off the last of her reservations. "Okay. Thanks, Tommy. I really appreciate it."

As she got in the car, as she pulled the door shut, she thought, somewhat flippantly, *I hope he's not a serial killer.*

Chapter 10

Charlie

Charlie Washington eyed the big round clock on the community room wall, his foot tapping in rhythm with the tense rap beat running through his head. It was 6:12, and Blake hadn't started the meeting yet. Charlie sighed inaudibly. He hadn't wanted to come to the library tonight. He was here to support his friend, that was all. But if the meeting didn't start soon, or if it dragged on for too long, he was out of here. He didn't have time for this crap.

Charlie had recently signed on as a game-tester for V-Play, an up-and-coming video game company, and he couldn't wait to get started. He loved video games and could hardly believe he was going to get paid for playing them. The first game had arrived on Tuesday, but Charlie hadn't had a chance to check it out. It had been a busy week, filled with extracurricular school activities, family obligations, and homework. He felt the game waiting for him, drawing him home like a drug he was already addicted to.

The room was strangely quiet. More than half of the attendees were occupied with their phones—texting friends, playing games, or scrolling through social media posts. Jared was slumped in his seat, dozing. Valentina wiggled her feet in front of her as she admired her own shoes, retro red pumps.

At 6:15, Blake shifted in his chair and said, "I guess no one else is coming, so we should probably get started. The library closes at seven on Fridays."

The turnout was sparse, eleven people out of the twenty-three who'd been in physics class on *would you rather* day. Charlie hadn't expected everyone to show up, but Blake obviously had. He'd arranged twenty-three folding chairs in a circle, like nursery school story time.

Charlie was surprised by how superstitious Blake and Ava were acting. They'd always been smart, practical people, but suddenly, they seemed to believe in black magic. Big deal, so Jared had won a thousand bucks and Reina had developed a case of alopecia. Hadn't they ever heard of coincidence? Even Deej and Will Rowland didn't seem that concerned, and they were two of the people who would die if their curses came true.

"So, we're here tonight to talk about the weird shit that's been going down since we played that game in physics class," Blake said. "Jared's lottery win, Reina's hair. Ava and I think the sub put a curse on us." His cheeks reddened slightly, as if he suddenly realized how crazy that sounded.

Jared, now wide awake, snorted. "What, you think one of the school's substitute teachers is an evil sorcerer or something?"

Blake shrugged.

Charlie said, "It's been almost two months since we played that game, and only two things have come true. Seems like coincidence to me."

"It could be," Blake conceded. "Or not. That's why

we need to discuss it."

He looked at Kylie Wentworth, who was fidgeting in her chair. "Kylie? Did you want to say something?"

Kylie looked nonplussed, like a victim of teacher cold-calling, but recovered quickly. "Just—Reina didn't start losing her hair till after that day. So, timing-wise, the curse thing adds up."

Reina wasn't present to speak for herself. After the wig debacle, she'd been so distraught that she'd gone to see the school nurse, who had sent her home. Charlie had heard about it from one of Reina's friends. For all he knew, Reina was still crying. Charlie had sisters. He knew how upset girls could get over their hair.

"In Jared's case, it might have been the power of suggestion," said DeShawn. He leaned forward, peering past Valentina to look at Jared. "Is that how it went down, bro? Did you decide to play the lottery *because* of that card?"

Jared scratched his shaggy blond head, and Charlie watched a few dandruff flakes flutter down onto his black sweatshirt. "Pretty much. So, my uncle and me, we're at the convenience store, and I see this lottery ticket display, and it makes me think of that card, how it said I would win a thousand bucks. And I'm like, 'Maybe today's the day.' So I asked Uncle Brad to buy me a ticket."

"There you go," said DeShawn, spreading his arms wide like he'd just solved the whole thing.

Blake said dubiously, "I mean, that's possible. But it's really strange. Most people who play the lottery don't win. And what are the odds that Jared would win the exact amount the card said he would win?"

"I agree," said Paisley. "I think we got cursed. The

whole time we were playing that game, I had this feeling of—of—" She gestured impotently.

"Doom," Ava and Kylie said at the same time.

"Yes, doom! And you know what else?" Paisley lowered her voice, and everybody leaned in to listen. "When I reached for a card, I accidentally bumped Mr. Trinkley's hand, and it was like this jolt of electricity shot through me."

"Oh my God! That happened to me, too," said Natalie Yoon. But she looked hopeful rather than horrified. Natalie had chosen *be able to read incredibly fast* over *be able to type incredibly fast* and was probably eager for her particular curse to kick in. Who wouldn't want to be able to skim through boring textbook chapters?

That raised a question in Charlie's mind. He said, "I wonder why some people got good destinies and others got bad ones."

"Yes!" said Paisley. "And why are some of the destinies just sort of bad while others are, like, 'You gonna die, dude'?"

Paisley's *would you rather* choice—swollen feet—fell into the just-sort-of-bad category.

"Good questions," said Blake. "I don't have the answers. Maybe Trinkley thought the randomness of the whole thing would make it more interesting."

Everyone went quiet for a few minutes, thinking their private thoughts. Natalie broke the silence. "If it really is a curse, I wonder how long it'll take for everything to come true. A couple of months? A year? Fifty years?"

"All I know is, mine's not going to happen anytime soon," Will Rowland said with a nervous laugh.

"Unless there's a guillotine in Pinedale I don't know about."

Will's card had given him the choice of getting decapitated or being poisoned to death. He'd chosen decapitation.

DeShawn quirked an eyebrow at him. "Guillotines aren't the only way to lose your head, bro. Maybe Maddy's serial killer is an ax murderer."

Blake wasn't sure if that was supposed to be a joke. Nobody laughed.

"Where is Maddy, anyway?" asked Deej. "Isn't she supposed to be here?"

"I talked to her after school," said Blake. "I think she was planning to come."

Deej's eyes drifted to the closed door, a small frown etching itself between his brows.

"My *would you rather* won't come true for a while either," said Charlie. When people looked at him blankly, he added, "I picked *land the perfect job*. That won't happen till I'm out of college."

Blake stared at him for a long moment. He said, "Dude. It already happened."

Ava gasped. "Oh my God, yes. The game-tester thing—that's a job!"

Charlie's heart rocketed in his chest as he realized his friends were right. At this stage of his life, being a video game tester was indeed the perfect job.

"So…that's three that have come true," Valentina said dazedly.

"Oh my God," screeched Lonnie Turko. "My mom's gonna die!"

Lonnie had been forced to choose between losing her mother and losing her father. She couldn't decide, so she'd flipped a coin.

Kylie said, "And Zoe's gonna freeze to death, and Deej is gonna die in a car accident, and Will's gonna get decapitated, and—and—" Her chest heaved like she was hyperventilating.

Will whimpered softly.

DeShawn stamped a foot on the fake-wood floor. "Guys! Let's not overreact. This doesn't necessarily mean anything."

"Or it could mean everything." Paisley dug around in her denim purse. "Where the hell is Maddy? I'm calling her."

All eyes were on Paisley as she clicked her phone on and tapped several keys. She pressed the phone to her ear and waited.

"Maddy? Hey, it's me." Charlie released a breath he hadn't realized he'd been holding. But a moment later a chill went through him as Paisley said, "Where are you? Call me right away."

Paisley wasn't talking to Maddy. She was talking to Maddy's voice mail.

"Text her stepsister," said Valentina.

Paisley's thumbs moved like crazy as she composed her message. Charlie heard a whoosh as she sent it on its way.

The reply came a few seconds later, its musical tone jarringly loud in the silent room. Paisley peered down at her phone. "Kristy says—she says Maddy left the house around 5:40." Her voice trembled, skimming the edges of hysteria. "She should have been here half an hour ago."

Everyone had the same look they'd had on *would you rather* day. The same look that was undoubtedly on

Charlie's face right now.

The look of fear.

At that moment, Alyssa burst through the door. "Sorry I'm late, guys. Mr. Prauss from school called me, and we were on the phone for, like, fifteen minutes."

When no one responded, she added, "You know— Mr. Prauss? The high school art teacher? Don't you guys wanna know what he wanted?" She giggled. "You won't believe it. *I* can hardly believe it. He was calling to tell me I won first place in a county art show!"

Chapter 11

Ava

Alyssa was a pretty girl—no one would dispute that. But when you looked into her pale blue eyes, you got the feeling there was nothing behind them but teddy bear stuffing.

Alyssa wasn't good at anything but being Alyssa. How had she won an art contest?

Ava knew how. It was in the cards—literally.

Blake filled Alyssa in on what had transpired so far, but Alyssa refused to believe there was a curse. "I probably had this talent all along but didn't realize it. I never really tried to do art before. But once I did, it was like, *wow!* I'm amazing!"

Jared said, "But Alyssa," and told the story of his winning lottery ticket. Alyssa rolled her eyes and said, "Lots of people win the lottery."

When Paisley reminded her that Maddy was missing, Alyssa said, "Just because you can't reach her doesn't mean she's missing."

When Blake mentioned Reina's hair loss, she'd had enough. "You guys are insane! There isn't any curse!" And she stormed out of the room.

Ava totally got it. If she'd unexpectedly developed a minor superpower, she might have felt the same way. She would want to believe the special ability was a product of her own grit and talent, not a malevolent gift thrust upon her by supernatural forces.

Paisley and Lonnie wept softly, overcome by everything they'd heard tonight. Ava tended to cry easily, too, especially when she had PMS, which happened to be the case today. But at the moment, she was too horrorstruck to do anything but gnaw on her thumbnail as she waited for Blake to get the meeting back on track. Blake was a smart, competent guy with a can-do attitude. He would have ideas on how to get them out of this.

She hoped.

Meanwhile, she needed to chill. She forced herself to breathe slowly while she thought things through. Even if her *would you rather* came true, even if she did go missing, it wouldn't necessarily be the end of the world. To everyone else, she would be missing, but she, Ava, would know where she was. Somehow, she would find her way back to her family.

Unless she was dead.

Or had amnesia.

Or was in the clutches of a serial killer, like Maddy.

The card hadn't revealed the circumstances of her disappearance. Anything could happen to her. Anything. She suddenly recalled that the card hadn't merely said *missing*. It had said *missing forever.*

She went back to being horrorstruck.

Blake finally got the meeting going again. "Does everybody agree that something freaky is going on? Something that isn't coincidence, isn't the power of suggestion, but something much worse?"

All around the circle, heads bobbed.

"Then let's start by getting organized. We need a volunteer to make a list of everyone in the class, which option they chose, and which fates have come true so far."

"I'll do it," said Ava. "I'll make a spreadsheet."

"Thanks, A. Also, we need to warn the others so they can take steps to save themselves."

Charlie gave him a dubious look. "Is that even possible? Won't the curse find a way no matter what?"

"Probably," said Blake. "Still, some people might be able to delay their fate, if not prevent it completely. Didn't Vishnu Singh have to choose between getting lost in the woods and getting lost in a bad section of the city?"

"Yeah, he picked the woods," said Deej.

"So we tell him to stay out of the woods."

"That won't work for everyone, though," said Kylie. "Liam Oswalt picked *break out in a grotesque rash*. I don't think that's preventable."

"That's why we need to find Mr. Trinkley," said Blake. "Maybe if we reason with him, he'll end the curse."

"How will we find him?" asked DeShawn.

Natalie waved a hand. "Mrs. Hendrickson in the school office should know how to reach him. I'll talk to her on Monday."

Paisley blotted her eyes with a tissue. "I don't understand any of this. Why does that guy hate us so much?"

"Maybe he doesn't," said Valentina. "Maybe he didn't know the cards were cursed." She glanced around at the skeptical faces of her classmates and amended, "That's probably not it, though."

"Well, whether he hates us or not, whether he knew about the curse or not, we're going to find him," said Blake. "And we will get to the bottom of this."

Ava appreciated Blake's optimism. She wasn't sure she shared it, but she definitely appreciated it.

After the meeting, the people with cars drove the walkers home. Nobody wanted to be out on the streets after dark, not with a serial killer on the loose. Ava caught a ride with Blake. They dropped Paisley off at her house and then headed for their own neighborhood. Along the way, they passed Maddy's house. A police car was in the driveway. Blake swung his car in behind it.

"Whoa. What are you doing?" asked Ava.

"We have to tell the police what we know." Blake switched the ignition off and opened his car door.

Ava grabbed his arm. "You're going to tell them about the curse? They'll never believe you."

"I have to try. Maddy's life is on the line."

Reluctantly, Ava followed him to the house. The front door was ajar, so they walked right in. Two officers from the Pinedale Police Department were in the living room—Officers Murphy and Rosenbaum. Officer Murphy, a beefy guy with the surly face of a bulldog, was on the couch talking to Maddy's mom, or trying to, anyway. Mrs. Eppley was crying so hard, Ava couldn't understand a word she said. Officer Rosenbaum, a tall, dark-haired lady who had *good cop* written all over her, was talking to Maddy's stepsister, Kristy. Maddy's stepfather sat on the other side of Maddy's mom, rubbing her back.

As Ava and Blake stepped into the living room, Officer Murphy looked up. "Who are you?"

"Um, friends of Maddy?" said Blake.

Mrs. Eppley half rose as she spotted them. "Blake, Ava—did you hear? My Maddy's gone missing!" She dropped back onto the couch as a fresh round of sobs seized her.

Officer Murphy strode over to Ava and Blake. "What are you kids doing here? Do you know where Madeline is?"

"Not exactly," said Blake. "We think she's been kidnapped by a serial killer."

"A serial killer! Oh my God!" shrieked Kristy. Mrs. Eppley cried harder than ever.

The cop's brown eyes blazed. "Son, you'd better have some real solid evidence to back up a claim like that."

Mrs. Eppley was wailing so loudly that it was hard to hear anything else. Officer Murphy led Ava and Blake into the kitchen. Ava tried not to cringe as Blake stammered out his tale. Mr. Trinkley, would you rather, the serial killer scenario, Jared's lottery win, Reina's hair. She heard the story through the cop's ears, heard how crazy it sounded, though she didn't think she could have told it any better.

Officer Murphy's scowl deepened as Blake continued to talk. Blake had just gotten to the part about Alyssa and the art contest when the cop slammed him against the wall.

"A girl is missing, and you're wasting my time with this bullshit?" He shook his head contemptuously. "I should arrest you right now for hindering an investigation."

"Sir, please listen," Ava said desperately. "We're only trying to help. We really think a serial killer kidnapped Maddy."

"A serial killer. Do you have any idea how unlikely that is? The vast majority of missing teenagers are runaways."

"Not Maddy," said Ava. "She would never run away."

Murphy released his grip on Blake and gave him a little shove. Blake staggered a few feet across the room before catching his balance.

"Where were you two tonight?" the cop asked, his shrewd eyes flicking from Blake to Ava. "Did you see Madeline? Were you with her?"

Blake shook his head. "We were supposed to be with her, but she never showed. That's why our friend Paisley texted Kristy."

"We were at the library," Ava added.

"Can anyone corroborate that?"

Corroborate. That was a big fancy police word, and Ava knew what it meant. The officer wondered if she and Blake had anything to do with Maddy's disappearance. "We were there with some classmates," she said. "The librarian saw us. Mrs. Berkebile. You can check with her."

Officer Murphy took down their names and addresses and the names of the other kids who'd been at the library and then shooed them out the door. Ava supposed they were lucky to have gotten away without being arrested.

Chapter 12

Valentina

Would you rather have nothing amazing ever happen to you, or have many amazing things happen, but each one is countered by an equally terrible event?

Valentina's *would you rather* question had been longer and clunkier than most, but she'd made her choice without hesitation. Bring on those amazing things! A bland, boring life would never do for Valentina Sanchez. She wasn't a vanilla kind of girl.

As for the terrible-event part—well, bad things were part of life. She would deal with her adversity like everybody else, though all those amazing things would surely soften the blows.

The first amazing thing came out of the blue on a random Monday, and it was a day she would never forget. Valentina had a major crush on the teen pop star Finn Rowdy and had been sending him fan letters for more than a year. She always included her phone number and invited him to call her if he ever wanted to talk.

Monday evening around six, her phone rang. She didn't recognize the number, though her phone said the call came from Los Angeles.

Los Angeles? That was where the stars lived!

She answered the call on the second ring with a

breathy "Hello?"

"Hi, is this Valentina?"

A warm flush spread over Val because the guy on the phone sounded exactly like Finn—that husky voice, the way he slurred his words as if slightly drunk. But of course that couldn't be. It had to be wishful thinking on her part, nothing more.

"Yeah, this is Val." She managed to keep her voice steady.

"Hi, Val, it's Finn. Finn Rowdy."

Something clunked so hard in her chest that she thought her heart had stopped beating. She tried to speak, but her vocal cords seemed to be paralyzed.

"Val, I get a lot of fan mail," said Finn Rowdy, "and I don't read most of it. But I read your recent letter, and I have to say, it touched me deeply. I can tell that you're a very special girl."

Val gulped. "Really?"

Then her brain started working again, and the hot flash subsided. Was she seriously supposed to believe that out of the thousands of fan letters Finn Rowdy received each week, he had zeroed in on hers and decided she was "special"?

Somebody was obviously pranking her, and Val thought she knew who. It had to be Deej Nolty, the class jokester. Deej knew about her celebrity crush—everyone did. He must have found somebody who could do a good Finn Rowdy impression and put him up to this.

"Tell Deej 'nice try,' " she said, and tapped the END CALL button.

Several seconds later, her phone rang again. Val was going to ignore the call, but when she glanced at her screen and saw that same location—*Los Angeles, CA*—she was suddenly filled with doubt. Finding someone who sounded like Finn Rowdy was one thing, but finding someone in Los Angeles? Did Deej even know anyone in LA?

Val answered the call. This time she didn't say hello. She just listened.

"Val? Look, I know it's hard to believe that a famous pop star would be calling you. I get it, I really do. How can I convince you?"

She thought for a moment. "Sing to me. Sing 'My Pasadena Pookie.' "

And so he did. Finn Rowdy, the famous pop star, sang his biggest hit to Valentina Sanchez, an ordinary teenager from Pinedale, North Carolina.

Val stood in front of her dresser mirror, watching her eyes get bigger and bigger as her jaw dropped lower and lower. She pointed at the phone pressed to her ear and mouthed *Finn Rowdy,* because she needed to tell someone the amazing news, and her reflection was the only other person in the room.

Finn said he would be doing a series of concerts in North Carolina in December and would like to send her tickets for one of them, along with a backstage pass. Maybe the two of them could go out for a bite to eat afterward. "I wanna get to know you better," he said in that smooth, mumbly voice.

After they hung up, Valentina burst out of her room, eager to tell her family the stunning news. She found her mom sitting at the kitchen table, her forehead propped against her hand. Crying hard.

"Wh—what's wrong?" asked Valentina.

Her mom took a big, hitching breath, trying to

collect herself. "It's Grandma Ellie."

Valentina had four biological grandparents and two step-grands. Of the six of them, Grandma Ellie, her mom's mom, was her favorite.

A flush crept over Val again, but it wasn't the same as the Finn Rowdy flush. It was more of a cold flush. A chill. "What about her?"

Her mom sobbed so hard, Valentina could barely understand her. "Your grandma's been diagnosed with terminal cancer!"

Chapter 13

Deej

Deej loved his dad, he really did, but sometimes he also hated him. Like today.

He scowled as he steered his quad into the field behind his house. The Sunday morning sunshine did nothing to brighten his mood.

It was the same pathetic story every week. Saturday night, his dad would drive to Raleigh to hit the bars. Sunday morning, Deej would wake up to find a strange woman in the house, and never the same one twice. These women seemed to adhere to a code of conduct that required them to dress scantily in the mornings. They'd show up in the kitchen wearing one of his dad's T-shirts that barely covered their asses, or a lacy bra and panties, or sometimes just the panties. They were never the least bit self-conscious when they encountered Deej, but that was okay because he was embarrassed enough for everybody.

Still, those floozies were nothing compared with the gem his dad had brought home last night. Deej hadn't even gotten a glimpse of her, though he'd heard the two of them having sex during the night. When he'd gotten up this morning, his dad was still in bed, which wasn't surprising. He tended to sleep till noon after one of his benders. But the girl? She was gone. And so was

Deej's laptop, his dad's tablet, and the cannister of cash they kept on top of the fridge.

Why did his dad have to be such an idiot? It was his fault Deej's mom had left, no doubt about it. She couldn't take the drinking, and Deej was pretty sure his dad had cheated on her, probably with the same type of woman he insisted on bringing home these days.

Yep, Duncan Nolty Sr. was an all-around loser. Deej supposed he should be grateful his dad wasn't bankrupt, which he surely would have been if he'd had a regular job. Because he wouldn't *have* a regular job— he would have been fired long ago. Duncan was employed by the family landscaping business, which had been started by Duncan's grandfather and was now run by his father and an uncle. He didn't do much actual work, though, and aside from an occasional disapproving frown or snarky comment, Duncan's dad and uncle seemed willing to let him slide. Enablers, that was what they were.

Life sucked. And it sucked even harder when Deej thought about Maddy. He was still trying to wrap his head around her disappearance. It hit him like a fist to the gut every time he thought about it. He'd cried during the candlelight vigil last weekend, something he hadn't done since he was little. Maddy had now been missing for eight days, and so far the police had no leads. They'd found her cell phone in the gutter two blocks from the library and said that foul play was likely.

It was funny, thought Deej, how you could know someone your whole life and suddenly see them in a different light. A romantic light. This feeling was brand-new, having flared up only since the beginning of the school year. And now Maddy had gotten herself kidnapped by a serial killer, and they would never get together. All because of *would you rather*.

Yep, life sucked.

Deej had come to terms with his own *would you rather* destiny. He considered himself one of the lucky ones, because he was pretty sure he could stave off death while he and his classmates figured out a way to break the curse. Forestalling his fate didn't seem that hard—in theory, anyway. He figured he was most likely to die as a passenger in his dad's car, considering that Duncan Senior was a hopeless alcoholic who drove drunk more than he drove sober. All Deej had to do to save himself was stay out of his dad's car. As an added precaution, he'd decided to forgo all cars for a while, not to mention trucks, vans, and buses.

He'd thought long and hard about the quad before deciding it didn't really qualify as a vehicle. It was more like a four-wheeled motorized bike. Besides, he used it primarily in the fields behind his house, where collisions were unlikely.

So everything was cool.

Except for the fact that life sucked.

He needed to be somewhere that would soothe his troubled soul, just till he mellowed out and thought up a way to pound some sense into his dad. He knew the perfect place, too—Bugbane Rock. There was a shortcut from here.

Named for the wild bugbane that grew nearby, Bugbane Rock was an idyllic spot in the patch of woods on the grounds of Pinedale Central High School, next to a lazy creek. Deej wasn't sure whether the "Rock" part of the name referred to the layers of slate on the forest floor or the rocky cliff that towered above them.

The school had kept the woods intact for practical reasons: biology classes often walked up there to collect nature specimens. But the area was used for other purposes, too. In the summertime, people picnicked on the broad, flat rocks at the creek's edge. Teenagers had clandestine beer parties there on balmy moonlit nights. Babies had been conceived at Bugbane Rock.

The cliff itself was a monolithic slab of stone the height of a three-story building. Some people said it was a meteorite that had fallen to earth millennia ago and partially embedded itself in a minor hillside. There was a ledge and a shallow cave near the top, but as far as Deej knew, nobody had been up there in years. Long ago, someone had fallen to their death, and afterward the path that led up to the ledge had been fenced off.

Deej snaked through a grove of trees and came out in a field on the other side, ignoring the big NO TRESPASSING sign. He was on Mr. Baldwin's property now, so he needed to be careful. Mr. Baldwin was a dick. In fact, his first name was Richard, so he really was a dick, ha-ha. Mr. B went berserk anytime he caught kids four-wheeling on his property. If he caught Deej, he would tell Deej's dad for sure and maybe even report him to the police. Deej pulled the hood of his sweatshirt up so he would be harder to recognize.

He didn't know what Mr. B's problem was. The guy didn't use this field for anything, so it wasn't like the four-wheeling was harming crops. Deej supposed some people just had it out for kids.

To reach the path into the woods, Deej had to drive dangerously close to Mr. B's house. He glanced toward the house as he approached. Shit! There was Mr. B coming out the back door, shaking his fist and shouting words Deej couldn't hear over the hum of the quad's motor. Swear words, no doubt. He gunned the throttle and zoomed toward the woods.

Whew! Safe. He followed the trail onto school grounds. Bugbane Rock was just up ahead. Deej zipped around a curve, and there on the path in front of him was a short, bearded man with overlarge ears and cool blue eyes.

Instinctively, he swerved to miss the man, the quad plowing through dense underbrush and mowing down tender saplings. He tried to slow down, but the throttle was jammed. He managed two thoughts before crashing into the rocky cliff wall.

(1) *Isn't that the creepy sub from physics class?*

(2) *Maybe the quad really is a vehicle.*

Chapter 14

Blake

Deej had been right about the closed casket. Blake wished the mortician had been able to make his friend presentable with makeup. He would have liked to see Deej's face one last time. But maybe it was better this way. Better to remember Deej the way he'd been than to stare down at a face that would never again flash that devilish smile.

The funeral home was packed. Sobbing girls, red-nosed boys, ashen-faced adults—the whole town had shown up to pay their respects. Flowers filled the room, and their commingled scents wafted up Blake's nose, as overpowering as his great-aunt Margaret's perfume.

Mr. Baldwin was there, strutting around and explaining himself to anyone who would listen.

"I seen him that day. On that ATV of his. Dang neighborhood kids got no respect for property lines. I tried to shoo him away, tried to get him off my land, but he ignored me, just like they all do. If he woulda turned around and gone home like I wanted, he'd be alive right now. Dang kids."

Blake wanted to shove the guy out of the funeral parlor and lock the door behind him.

He wound his way over to Ava, who stood alone in a corner blowing her nose. Ava's eyes were red and swollen. Her hair was matted, and she wasn't exuding her usual delectable strawberry scent, which made him think she hadn't showered today. Not that he was judging. Grief did funny things to people.

"Well. That's the end of the Alphabet Quartet," Ava said in a quavery voice.

"Still, we have to go on," said Blake. "Deej would want us to. We can be—I don't know. The ABC Three."

Ava gave a bitter laugh. "Until I disappear. Then you'll be down to the BC Two."

Blake wasn't sure how to respond to that, so he clamped his mouth shut. He didn't want to make Ava mad by saying the wrong thing.

"We need to tell somebody," Ava said. "An adult, someone who can help us solve this. I was thinking Principal Kouriki."

"No." Blake was adamant. "You saw Officer Murphy's reaction. He didn't believe me. You think Kouriki would be any different?"

"At least she would hear us out."

Blake shook his head.

"Then how about Mr. Copeland? He's the guidance counselor. Helping students is his job."

"Mr. Copeland helps kids pick the right classes and deal with bullies. Do you really think he knows how to end a curse?"

"We have to do *something*. Deej died, Blake! And more people will die if we don't stop the curse. We can't handle this by ourselves anymore."

Blake sighed. "I don't know. Let me think about it."

Ava glanced around the crowded room. "Oh.

Hank's here."

Blake followed her gaze and saw Pinedale Central High's daytime custodian hovering in the doorway like he wasn't sure he should come in. "Let's go talk to him. Maybe he knows Mr. Trinkley."

Natalie had asked Mrs. Hendrickson in the school office how to contact Mr. Trinkley, but Mrs. Hendrickson had been no help at all. In fact, she'd been downright snippy. Natalie had gotten the feeling there was some sort of weirdness surrounding Mr. Trinkley's stint as a sub, but Mrs. Hendrickson wouldn't talk.

"Um…" Ava shrank away from Blake. "Do we have to?"

"Yes, Ava. We have to."

Ava had some weird notions about Hank. She thought he was creepy and quirky and secretive, though that was just her wild imagination asserting itself. There was nothing wrong with Hank, nothing at all. Blake had always liked the guy.

Hank wore a faded blue dress shirt that strained against his plump belly. Blake expected buttons to pop off at any second. The shirt was probably a remnant from his thinner days, and—who knew?—maybe he didn't have anything nicer to wear to a funeral home.

Blake maneuvered his way across the room, Ava plodding along behind him. Twice he had to stop and wait for her to catch up. Finally they reached the custodian. Blake said, "Hank, hi. I'm glad you came."

Hank gave his head a mournful shake. "Big shame, what happened to young Duncan. Been too much tragedy around here lately. Three separate incidents in a little over a week—that's a lot for a town as small as Pinedale."

Blake started to nod but stopped as Hank's words sank into his brain. "Three incidents? I only know about two—Maddy and Deej. What's the third?"

Hank puffed up a little, as if pleased to be the bearer of news. "It happened this morning. Freak accident involving Officer Murphy, the cop in charge of investigating the Eppley girl's disappearance."

Ava's eyes were huge. "What happened?"

"Tree branch fell on his head as he was walking to his cruiser. He's in a coma. The doctors don't think he'll ever wake up."

"That's awful!" said Blake. Ava threw him a look, but he couldn't decipher it.

Hank agreed about the awfulness of the situation, and the three of them bowed their heads in an impromptu moment of silence.

When Blake felt that enough time had passed, he opened his mouth to ask Hank about Mr. Trinkley. But before he could get any words out, Hank spoke.

"Ah, there's Steve—Duncan Junior's grandpap. Steve and me go way back. If you'll excuse me, I should go over and offer my condolences." He brushed past Blake and Ava.

"Well, how about that," Blake said, giving Ava a dry look. "We survived an encounter with Hank the Werewolf, or Hank the Space Alien, or whatever the heck you think he is."

Ava ignored that. She pulled Blake to an out-of-the-way spot next to a table crowded with flowers and said, "You're right, B. Telling people about the curse is a bad idea."

If he hadn't been so grief-stricken over Deej, Blake might have smiled. "I'm glad you see it my way. But why the change of heart?"

"You told Officer Murphy about the curse, and now he's in a coma. Don't you get it? The curse doesn't want us to tell others about it. Anybody we tell will be cursed, too, only they won't get to choose their fate. The curse will decide for them."

Blake didn't know if Ava was right—it was tough to make a sound deduction based on one guy in a coma—but his gut told him she was. "Have you told anybody about the curse?"

Ava shook her head. "I almost told my dad. But then I got this funny feeling that I shouldn't."

"Yeah." Blake had started to tell his brother but had stopped when he'd gotten that same funny feeling. "We should warn the others. Let's hope everybody's been keeping their mouths shut."

A bunch of the *would you rather* kids were shambling around looking shell-shocked. It was now crystal-clear that the curse meant business. It wasn't going to back down. If Deej could die, others could, too, and it was impossible to know who would be next.

Blake and Ava drifted through the crowd, telling their classmates what had happened to Officer Murphy. Luckily, no one had talked. They'd all had that same instinct to keep the curse to themselves. Blake wished he hadn't ignored that feeling when he'd spoken to Officer Murphy.

As he moved through the crowd, he kept one eye on Hank, intending to continue their conversation once Hank was done talking to Deej's grandpa. He saw the two men hugging. But when he looked back a few seconds later, Hank was gone.

"Where'd he go?" he asked Ava, craning his head

wildly in multiple directions.

"Where'd who go?"

"Hank."

Ava took a quick look around. "I don't see him. He must have left."

"That's impossible. I was watching him. He was with Deej's grandpa a second ago, and now he's gone. There's no way he could have gone out the door that fast."

"Well, obviously he did. But look." She pointed to a spot near Deej's casket. "Mr. Perry is here. He's been at the school almost as long as Hank. He might know something about Mr. Trinkley."

Mr. Perry taught French at Pinedale Central High School. Unlike Hank, he was slim and fit and had most of his hair—which, granted, was gray. Mr. P had a ready smile and a hearty laugh, though his eyes held a hint of sadness. Blake remembered hearing that Mr. P's wife had died a few years back.

"I'm so sorry about your friend," Mr. Perry said when Blake and Ava reached him. "What a tragic loss."

Blake's throat swelled with a fresh wave of grief. "Yeah."

"I always liked Deej," Mr. Perry went on. "Personally, I enjoyed his rascally sense of humor. He reminded me of myself as a boy."

They chatted about Deej for a few minutes. Then Ava said, "We need to ask you something."

"Ask away," said Mr. Perry.

"We had a substitute teacher at the beginning of the school year and were wondering if you know him. Mr. Trinkley?"

Mr. Perry stroked his chin as he pondered that.

"Trinkley? I can't say I recall a sub by that name. The only Trinkley I ever knew was a man who taught at the school many years ago. Larry Trinkley."

"How long ago?" asked Blake. "Is it possible he came back as a sub?"

Mr. Perry gave a laugh that had no mirth in it. "No. Larry barely had a year in at the school when he died in a tragic accident. I always liked the man. We shared an interest in skeet shooting, so we had that to talk about. But Larry wasn't popular with his students. Tough grader, didn't put up with any nonsense."

"Oh. So he's dead," Blake said. For a second he'd thought maybe they were getting somewhere. He should have known it wouldn't be that easy.

"Yes, quite dead," said Mr. P. "In fact—" His eyes wandered to Deej's casket. "Larry died at the same spot where Deej died. Bugbane Rock. That's an odd coincidence, now isn't it?"

Chapter 15

Maddy

The cellar was a lot like Maddy's cellar at home—cold, dim, and dank. Concrete floor, concrete-block walls, a spider in every corner. The place reeked of mildew, and with every breath, Maddy imagined mold spores rushing up her nostrils. That couldn't be good for her health. If she had to be imprisoned, she wished it was in an above-ground bedroom, or at least an attic. She would have settled for an attic.

Well, at least she hadn't been murdered—not yet, anyway. She hadn't even been raped. As kidnappers went, Tommy wasn't so bad. He provided three decent meals a day. Her bed was a mattress on the floor, but it was comfortable and included a soft pillow and warm covers. A bucket for a bathroom—that was the worst part. She got embarrassed every time Tommy came to empty it, but he didn't seem to mind.

She'd lost track of time but knew she'd been here for more than a week. She'd been hysterical the first few days, and Tommy's frown had told her he didn't like that at all. Aside from bringing meals and emptying the poop bucket, he'd pretty much left her alone. But now that she'd calmed down, he came to the cellar more often. Sometimes they played cards or checkers. Sometimes they talked.

Maddy let Tommy do most of the talking as she tried to figure him out. She filed every bit of information away in a folder in her brain. Maybe she could use that knowledge to find a way out of this nightmare. There was no wife—she knew that now. Sometimes he talked about his mother, but always in the past tense, which led Maddy to believe the woman was dead. She was pretty sure Tommy lived here alone, wherever *here* was.

She assessed her surroundings as best she could. There wasn't much noise from outside. No barking dogs or squealing children, just muted bird twitter and the occasional rumble of a passing car in the distance. Maddy was pretty sure the house was in a secluded area. She'd done a lot of screaming in those early days, and Tommy had made no effort to silence her. Clearly, he hadn't been worried that someone would hear her.

There were two windows set high on one of the cellar walls. Plain brown paper was taped across each one, thick enough to block curious eyes but not so opaque that light couldn't get through. The windows were approximately two-and-a-half feet wide by twelve inches high, big enough for her to fit through. But when the sun shone at a certain angle, it made a striped pattern on the brown paper that told her there were bars on the outsides of those windows.

Tommy was gone for a good chunk of most days, which suggested he had a job. But it wasn't always the same chunk of time, which indicated shiftwork. Maddy suspected that he worked in a store, because sometimes he mentioned *customers* and *merchandise*. She knew now that he didn't work with her mom. He must have been a patron in the diner at some point and heard her and her mom talking. That was how he'd learned their names. It was also why he looked familiar.

Would she ever see her family again? She clung to that hope. Every day she reminded herself that the *would you rather* card hadn't said she would be murdered by a serial killer. It had only said *kidnapped.*

And every day her resident pessimist reminded her that the card hadn't ruled out murder, either.

She could only imagine the hell her mom was going through. Her stepdad and stepsister, too.

There'd never been a real dad in the picture. Every time she asked her mom who her father was, Laura got a deer-in-the-headlights look that made Maddy think she didn't know. Her mother had apparently been pretty wild in her younger days. Ick, Maddy didn't like to think about that. Anyway, it didn't matter, because now she had Ron, stepfather extraordinaire. Although he was Kristy's biological dad, not Maddy's, he gave the girls equal amounts of love and attention.

Ron's love for Laura was also apparent. Maddy saw it in the way he looked at her, in the things he did for her, and in the gifts he brought her—candy and flowers and jewelry, uninspired but sweet. Ron and Laura had been together for almost three years, and Maddy had never seen her mom so happy. Actually, she'd never seen her mom happy at all, not really. Even now, with Ron in her life, her eyes always had a haunted look.

Maddy had known from an early age that her mom wasn't like other moms. She never laughed, seldom smiled, and Maddy had lost track of how many times she'd caught Laura crying softly in her bedroom. Something troubled her, something from her past, and

Maddy had a feeling it was a lot worse than bearing a child out of wedlock. She'd repeatedly demanded to know what was wrong, but Laura refused to tell her.

Now she would never learn her mother's secret—unless she escaped from Tommy.

She spent her days prowling around the cellar, searching for anything that might be of use. But her searches were fruitless. The cellar had been scrubbed clean of everything but her prison furnishings: the mattress, the bucket, a card table, two folding chairs, and a small TV with a built-in DVD player. A couple of movies, too, all from the 2000s. There was a laundry sink where she took sponge baths and washed her hair, but no washer or dryer. Opposite the windows was a padlocked wooden door, its green paint peeling badly. Maddy had asked Tommy what was inside, but Tommy had ignored the question.

She'd found something chilling at the bottom of that door—names scratched into the wood. Sarah, Marni, Brooke. Her predecessors. She wondered how long the girls had been kept in the cellar before—

She could never bear to finish that thought.

Still, she found hope in the presence of those names. They'd been scratched into the wood with *something*, a tool of some sort. Not metal silverware—Tommy never gave her anything but plastic utensils for her meals, and she assumed that had been true for the others. Was there a knife or a screwdriver hidden somewhere in the cellar? If so, it was well concealed.

She would keep looking. What did she have to lose?

Chapter 16

Ava

Charlie and Ava had a fifth-period study hall together in Mrs. Martinetti's room. Mrs. Martinetti taught computer science, and she was one of the nicest teachers in the school. She didn't mind if people talked or played with their phones or even moved around the classroom, as long as they did it quietly.

Ava liked the way Mrs. Martinetti's eyes crinkled in her doughy face when she smiled. She admired Mrs. Martinetti's lustrous brown hair, those apple-dumpling cheeks. She had never hugged Mrs. Martinetti but imagined that doing so would be like wrapping your arms around a large, comfortable pillow.

Ava and Charlie sequestered themselves in a rear corner of the classroom for a private conversation.

"Somebody told me Zoe Malinowsky went to Miami to live with her dad," said Charlie. "Is that true?"

Ava nodded. "She figures she has less of a chance of freezing to death there."

"I haven't heard any updates since yesterday. Has anybody else's fate come true?"

"Yeah." Ava wrinkled her nose. "Ben Lawrence."

"Remind me what he picked?"

"Ben had to choose between chronic b.o. and

breath that smells like rotting garbage. He picked rotting garbage."

"Ah, right. So his breath is bad?"

Ava gave him a deadpan look. "Dude, you have no idea. It flared up for the first time today in English class. Ben sits three rows over from me, but the smell was so strong I felt like I was trapped inside a garbage truck. People were gagging. Mrs. Pelegrino sent him to see the school nurse."

"Poor Ben."

"Also, Kylie's fate might be coming true. She picked *lose your best friend* over *lose all your friends except your best friend*, and now Kalisha isn't speaking to her."

"Uh-oh. Those two have been besties forever. What happened?"

"Kalisha won't say. I asked her, but all she said was, 'She knows what she did.' Kylie has no clue. She swears she didn't do anything."

Many of their classmates were going through hellish times. Now that their group had acknowledged the curse, it seemed to be coming at them full-force, like a ravenous tiger.

"I feel bad that I got such a good fate," said Charlie.

"No, you don't." The words slipped out before Ava could stop them, and in an uncharacteristically waspish tone. Charlie looked at her like she'd suddenly shape-shifted into a two-headed ogre.

Well, the statement couldn't be unsaid, and the sentiment was one she'd felt for a while, so she might as well follow through. "The curse has been good to you, Charlie. Don't deny it. You're having a blast testing video games."

Charlie dropped his gaze, but not before Ava saw the hurt in his eyes. "Sure, the games are fun, but that doesn't mean I'm glad about the curse. Let me try again. I'm sorry so many people got bad fates. Especially you. I wish the curse had never happened. There, is that better?"

He looked at her, his face raw and honest, and Ava wished she hadn't lashed out. None of this was his fault. "I'm sorry, C," she said, reaching out to clasp his hand. "I'm just pissed because you get to play video games while I'm on the brink of disappearing."

"It's cool," said Charlie. "I'd be pissed, too. And I'd probably be a hell of a lot meaner than you're being."

Ava granted him a small smile.

"We have to find Mr. Trinkley," said Charlie. "It's our only hope of ending the curse."

"How can we find him? Mrs. Hendrickson was no help. Mr. Perry never heard of the guy. We're at a dead end."

"You don't want to talk to Kouriki?"

"No. She'd want to know why we're so interested in some random sub. She would hound us till we spilled the whole story."

"Has anyone tried an internet search?"

"How would that help? We don't even know the guy's first name."

"Still. It's worth a try." Charlie glanced toward the front of the room, where Mrs. Martinetti sat at her desk, chatting with Stef Abramson. "Why don't we do it now?"

They told Mrs. Martinetti they were working on a

project and needed to go to the library to do research. They could have used one of the computers in Mrs. Martinetti's room, but Ava thought they would have more privacy in the library. Mrs. Martinetti cheerfully gave them passes, and they went on their way.

There were only a few students in the library. Ava and Charlie headed to the back and seated themselves at a computer. Charlie opened a search engine and typed, "Substitute teacher Trinkley, Pinedale NC."

A slew of results came up. The first few were articles on how to become a substitute teacher. Then came articles about people named Trinkley who didn't necessarily live in Pinedale, followed by articles about Pinedale that didn't mention anyone named Trinkley.

They would have to comb through the results one by one. It would be a needle-in-a-haystack search, and there might not even be a needle.

Charlie scrolled slowly down the page.

"Oh." Ava jabbed a forefinger at one of the listings. "This sounds like the guy Mr. Perry knew."

The heading read: *Pinedale Teacher Dies in Tragic Accident.*

Charlie clicked on the link, and a news article bloomed to life on the computer screen. Simultaneously, Ava and Charlie gasped.

At the top of the page was a photograph of the man who had cursed them.

Ava studied the photo, noting the guy's close-cropped beard and large ears. The photo was black and white, but she could tell his eyes were blue. The resemblance to their Mr. Trinkley was uncanny.

Charlie slumped against the back of his chair. "So I guess this means…it means—what? That this guy is our

Mr. Trinkley's dad?" He blew out a forceful breath. "That's wild. I mean, people say I look like my dad. Same eyes, same chin, we even walk the same. But Dad and me, what we got is nothing like this. We have our similarities but also our differences. My face is thinner. His eyebrows are shaggier. But this guy? He could be the other Mr. Trinkley's clone."

Ava sat quietly while he prattled on. When he was done, she said, "This isn't a case of family resemblance, C. It isn't a case of cloning. Don't you realize what's going on?"

She watched him think it over. She watched the horror dawn in his eyes. When he spoke, his voice was no more than a cracked whisper. "This is him. This is the guy who cursed us. He's a ghost."

Chapter 17

Blake

Charlie called an after-school meeting of the *would you rather* group. Seventeen people met up in a little-used side hallway near the gym.

"Got some tea to spill," said Charlie, not wasting any time. Everyone was lined up along the wall while Charlie paced in front of them like a military leader. He told the group about the internet search he and Ava had done. He announced that Mr. Trinkley was a ghost.

This wasn't news to Blake. He'd heard about it from Ava when he'd run into her before seventh period. Apparently, everyone else had heard, too. People looked troubled but not really surprised. Anyway, he'd always suspected the school was haunted, even though Principal Kouriki insisted it wasn't. Blake knew a number of kids who claimed to have seen ghosts at Pinedale Central High School.

Charlie had the article about Trinkley's fatal accident pulled up on his phone. Scrolling through it, he said, "Trinkley was killed at Bugbane Rock. Two hikers found his body on the rocks below the cliff. The medical examiner determined that he died from blunt force trauma, and the logical assumption was that he'd fallen from the cliff. But nobody could figure out why he'd gone there alone after school or what he was doing on the cliff."

Ava said, "Can you text the article link to everybody? Well—everybody except Blake."

"Sure," said Charlie. He gave Blake a sympathetic glance. "Sorry, man. I'll email it to you."

It had finally happened. Yesterday, Blake's cell phone had gone missing. The disappearance had occurred swiftly and without fanfare—the phone had been in his backpack at the beginning of French class and gone at the end. He'd checked and rechecked his backpack, retraced his steps, talked to Mr. Perry, and searched the lost-and-found box in the school office, all to no avail. It was as if his phone had flown to the moon and buried itself in a crater.

His mom had scolded him for his carelessness and said that if he wanted a new phone, he would have to buy it himself. Blake couldn't afford the model he'd had previously, so he'd purchased a cheap burner phone, the kind you had to buy minutes for.

Then that phone had gone missing, too.

So he'd resigned himself to being phone-free, at least until the curse ended. Assuming it could be ended.

Charlie continued, "Ava and I looked Trinkley up in the school yearbook from twenty years ago. There's an In Memoriam page that gives the dates of his birth and death. The day we played *would you rather* was the twentieth anniversary of his death."

"What does it all mean?" asked Valentina.

Nobody had an answer.

"I can't believe he's a ghost," said Paisley. "Ghosts are usually see-through, right? But this guy was solid. He looked like a living person. How did he do that?"

Blake tried to look at Paisley's face as she spoke,

but his eyes kept drifting to her feet. They were so swollen, they looked like shapeless red bricks. None of her shoes fit, so she'd taken to wearing huge, furry bedroom slippers. But even the slippers were too tight, so she went barefoot most of the time.

"The bigger question is why he cursed us," said DeShawn.

"Only one person knows the answer to that," said Charlie. "And he's dead."

A collective sigh went through the group. Ava stepped away from the wall and said, "We need to hold a séance."

Several people nodded, while others milled around looking terrified. Charlie said, "That's a great idea, A. Let the guy himself explain why he's doing this. Maybe if we ask nicely, he'll end the curse."

Lonnie said to Brianna, "There's something on your neck. A reddish-brown speck…" She peered closer. "…with legs."

Brianna swatted at her neck. "It's a bedbug. My house is infested with them."

Lonnie edged away. So did everyone else who'd been standing near Brianna, including Natalie Yoon, whose friendship with Brianna had recently blossomed into something more. Nothing like a bug infestation to put a damper on romance, thought Blake.

"It was either that or spiders," Brianna went on, glancing around the group as if looking for absolution. "I thought this would be better."

Heels tapped briskly in the corridor around the corner. Blake knew that tap, and he knew that gait. Principal Kouriki was coming. Charlie held a forefinger to his lips, urging everyone to be quiet. Unfortunately, there was nowhere to hide. Principal Kouriki rounded the corner and came to an abrupt halt when she saw them.

"What are you kids doing down here? School let out half an hour ago. Is there a sporting event I don't know about?"

"Um, we formed a jogging club," said Ava, the quickest thinker among them. "It's not through the school or anything. We just discovered we all like to run, so we arranged to meet here to get started. We were about to go outside and do laps around the building."

"In your school clothes?" The principal's glance landed pointedly on Valentina's chunky-heeled fashion boots and Kylie's metallic flats. "And on a day when it's going to rain?"

"Dang!" said DeShawn, a little too heartily. "We should have checked the weather forecast. Guess we'll have to reschedule."

Kouriki's shrewd gaze swept around the group, landing on each person in turn. Blake stared down at Charlie's orange and blue sneakers to avoid meeting her eyes. It was rumored that Kouriki could read minds.

"A lot of strange things have been happening around here lately," the principal said. "Tragedies, victories. Bizarre health conditions." Her eyes lingered on Paisley's feet before moving to Ben Lawrence, who stood twenty feet away popping breath mints into his mouth. "One might almost think something more than coincidence is at play."

She raised her eyebrows, waiting for a response.

A minute went by. Jared Crofton gave a one-shouldered shrug and said, "Shit happens."

Principal Kouriki didn't yell at him for using bad language. She just said, "Well. If any of you ever want to talk, and I sincerely hope you will, you know where to find me. Now get out of here. School's over for the day." And she went tapping on down the hall.

"We should tell her everything," Lonnie said desperately. "Maybe she can help. Because if we don't break the curse, my mom's gonna die!"

Blake's eyes settled on Principal Kouriki's departing back. He almost called out to her. He almost agreed to spill the whole terrible story, because Lonnie was right—Kouriki might know what to do. This was her school. *Would you rather* had happened on her watch. She was pretty much obligated to find a way out of it.

But he kept his mouth shut. Telling her about the curse would only doom her like the rest of them. Kouriki would get mauled to death by an escaped zoo lion or crushed to death by a falling piano or suffer some other horrible fate. And her blood would be on Blake's hands.

"I'm sorry, Lonnie. We can't," he said. "But I think we have a good chance of getting somewhere with the séance."

Lonnie burst into tears.

"Let's do the séance tomorrow night," said Ava. "The yearbook says Mr. Trinkley was a math teacher, and he taught in classroom 211. We'll meet there at eight o'clock."

"I'm not sure I can come," said Valentina. The way her eyes darted around told Blake she was scared. Really scared.

"That's fine," said Ava. "We only need a few

people. Four would be perfect. I'll be one of them. Anybody else willing to commit?"

Blake, Charlie, and Kylie volunteered.

"How will we get into the building?" asked Kylie.

Charlie said, "The night janitor usually leaves the door at the rear of the science wing unlocked. I sneak in that way all the time to get things from my locker after school hours. We just have to make sure to keep out of sight."

"Okay then. We have a plan," said Blake. But he couldn't help wondering what he'd gotten himself into. What if Trinkley's ghost inflicted something worse than a missing cell phone on him?

Chapter 18

DeShawn

Charlie offered to drive DeShawn home from the meeting, but DeShawn declined. Home wasn't where he was headed. He knew Charlie would have given him a ride no matter where he was going, but he didn't want Charlie—or anyone else, for that matter—to know about his destination.

DeShawn was on his way to Jade Zimmer's house. Over the past few weeks, he'd been nurturing a thing with her, a tiny flame that he hoped to coax into a bonfire. Jade sat behind him in homeroom, and every morning they talked, joked, bantered, flirted—all that ritualistic pre-ship stuff. Sometimes she twirled her pencil through his dreadlocks. Sometimes he dropped chocolate kiss candies on her desk.

He hadn't told anybody he liked Jade, not even Will Rowland, his best friend, because he didn't want to jinx his chances of getting with her. He knew how these things went. You confided in a friend, but the friend couldn't keep their mouth shut, and pretty soon the whole school knew, including your love interest, who was so mortified by all the teasing that she wanted nothing further to do with you.

DeShawn had been down that road more than once. But not this time. This time he'd managed to keep his own secret, and things had been going well with Jade. (He thought.) Tonight, if everything went according to plan, he would lock in a date for the Christmas dance. Jade really wanted to go. She'd talked about the dance a lot over the past week and as recently as this morning had said she didn't yet have a date. Was that a hint? DeShawn thought so.

A fat raindrop splattered on his head. He shot a glance toward the roiling gray clouds overhead. Principal Kouriki had said it was going to rain, and when Kouriki said something would happen, it usually did. The birds seemed to know bad weather was coming. A small flock of them circled overhead, squawking like crazy.

DeShawn walked faster, hoping to make it to Jade's house before the sprinkles intensified into a downpour. Raindrops pelted him sporadically, landing mostly on his head and shoulders. It was an odd rain, though. He didn't see any droplets slicing through the air, and the ground remained dry. It seemed to be raining mostly on him.

He rounded a corner, and there was Jade's house up ahead, a stately two-story with fancy brick pillars flanking the mouth of the driveway. DeShawn trotted up the porch steps and rang the doorbell. After a minute, the door swung open, revealing a large Black man with a buzz cut. Jade's dad. The man took his glasses off and frowned down at him. DeShawn swallowed hard, already intimidated.

"Hi! Is Jade here? I'm her friend DeShawn, from school."

"Yes, Jade's here." The man had a deep, authoritative voice. "But you are not coming into my house like that."

DeShawn gaped in confusion. "Wh—what do you mean?"

Jade's dad planted his fists on his hips and spoke in an incredulous tone. "Young man, you are covered in bird crap!"

DeShawn reached up to touch a wet spot on his head. His fingers came away coated in a pasty white substance.

All those wet splooshes he'd felt? They hadn't been rain after all.

"Shit!" he muttered. Instantly, he clamped a hand over his mouth—the one that didn't have bird poop on it. "Sorry!"

Had a teenage boy ever made a worst first impression on a girl's father?

"It's okay," said Mr. Zimmer. "That's—that's a very apt expletive, actually." The corners of his mouth twitched. He seemed to be struggling to contain himself as his eyes lingered on DeShawn's head. The struggle didn't last long. Suddenly he was laughing. Laughing hard.

DeShawn gave a sheepish grin, though he felt more like crying.

Would you rather had finally caught up with him. He'd been dreading it for so long, it was almost a relief to find that his day of reckoning had arrived.

The options on his card had been unpleasant but not lethal: *Would you rather receive a painful shock each time you touch metal or be pooped on by birds every time you go outside?* His classmates had snickered, but DeShawn had approached the scenario with the same logic and gravity he would have used to purchase a car.

Painful shock seemed to be the worse option. He'd tried to add up all the metal in his life—computers and cars and phones and bikes and keys and silverware and soda cans and nail clippers and doorknobs and scissors and paperclips and coins and probably a zillion other things he hadn't been able to think of at that moment. He would receive hundreds of shocks each day, presumably for the rest of his life.

Getting pooped on by birds, though—that was something he could control. To avoid it, he could simply stay indoors. When he had to go outside, he would take an umbrella. He imagined a handful of neighborhood birds waiting for him to emerge from his house each morning, taking their obligatory dump, and then going on their way. Now he saw that he wasn't going to get off that easy. He'd been bombarded by wet splats the whole way to Jade's house, which suggested the onslaught would continue as long as he stayed outdoors. The entire avian population of Pinedale must be in on it. Maybe the whole world.

"How—how did this happen?" Jade's dad asked. His words came out between hysterical wheezes. "I have to say—in my entire life—I have never once—been shit upon by a bird!" *Hahahahaha. S*o much laughing. DeShawn was getting seriously annoyed.

"I don't know, sir," he said tersely. "It just happened." A blob of bird poop slid down his temple.

Finally, Mr. Zimmer got himself under control. He wiped his eyes and put his glasses back on. "Tell you what. There's a faucet at the rear of the house, under the deck. You can rinse your head off there. Leave your jacket on the porch. Then you can come in." He winked. "Don't worry; I won't tell Jade." The cackling started up again as he shut the door.

The water gushing out of the faucet was ice-cold. DeShawn scrubbed his head until his scalp and fingers were numb. He rinsed his dangling dreadlocks and then pulled a few strands in front of his face to inspect them. The white goo was deeply embedded. He didn't know if it would ever come out.

When he'd cleaned himself up as best he could, he returned to Jade's porch. He removed his jacket and rang the doorbell.

This time Jade answered the door. She looked startled to see him. "DeShawn, hey."

"I was in the neighborhood," said DeShawn, wincing at his own cliché. "Thought I'd stop by to see what you're up to."

"What I'm up to," Jade repeated flatly. "Well, I finally got a date for the Christmas dance. I guess that's what I'm up to."

All the breath whooshed out of DeShawn. He croaked, "What?"

"I'm going with Drew Sanderson. He just texted me a few minutes ago."

DeShawn managed not to WTF her—but seriously? Drew Sanderson? The kid was a conceited jerk, not to mention a real Chad. Oh, the anguish, the fury! Wasn't it enough that he had birds pooping on his head? Did they have to poop on his heart, too?

It was all because of that damned curse. If he hadn't had to scrub his head, if he'd gotten to Jade a little sooner, he could have asked her to the dance before Drew swooped in and ruined his life.

"He's in my English class," Jade went on,

sounding slightly defensive. "I don't know him that well, but sometimes we talk." Her voice went down to a mumble. "I just really wanted to go to the dance."

"Well, now you get to," said DeShawn.

He'd planned to ask Jade to the dance yesterday in homeroom but had lost his nerve when he'd noticed Brandon Rucker, who sat across from him, unabashedly listening in. He'd almost asked her today, at her locker, but then two of her friends had rushed up and bumped him out of the way. He'd finally decided it would be easier—and classier—to ring her doorbell and do the asking in the privacy of her home. By this time the venture felt as weighty as a marriage proposal.

And now he'd been beaten out by a guy who used text messaging to invite girls to dances. What a classless jerk. Although Drew wasn't part of the *would you rather* group, DeShawn wished a horrible fate upon him—life in prison or uncontrollable farting or something.

Jade was looking at him in a weird, pensive way, like she knew how close they'd come to making a date for the Christmas dance. If she would say, "You know, I really wanted to go to that dance with you," or if DeShawn would say, "I came here tonight to ask you to the dance," it would be out in the open. They could talk about it, figure out what had gone wrong, and decide where to go from there.

But neither of them said those things, so the weird look in Jade's eyes stayed in her eyes. For a little while, anyway. As it faded, she asked, "What's that white stuff in your dreads? Paint?"

That was as good of an explanation as any. "Yeah. I'm helping my dad paint my sister's bedroom furniture."

Jade opened the door wider. "It's chilly out there. You wanna come in?"

DeShawn hesitated. He wasn't sure about the proper protocol for this situation. Were Jade and Drew now an official thing? Would Drew be pissed if he found out DeShawn had hung out at her house?

He took a step backward. "I should probably get home. Lots more furniture to paint. I just wanted to say hi."

"Well, then—hi." She stared down at the porch floor, a brooding look on her pretty face. "I guess I'll see you tomorrow in homeroom."

DeShawn grabbed his jacket and took off.

Bird poop rained down on him the whole way home. He wished he'd asked Jade for an umbrella.

Chapter 19

Ava

Ava's grandparents played bingo at the United Methodist Church every Wednesday night from seven until nine. That gave Ava the perfect opportunity to enter their house and fetch Gram's old spirit board from the attic. She was only borrowing it, but it was best if the grands didn't know. Otherwise there would be questions she wasn't prepared to answer.

After leaving the house, she returned the spare key to the fake rock under the porch and trotted to the car where Blake, Charlie, and Kylie waited. When she got into the front seat, Charlie said, "I feel like a getaway driver."

Ava laughed, but it was a nervous laugh. She had no idea what was in store for them tonight.

Parking at the school was out of the question because what if the night janitor saw the car? He would come looking for them and would probably report them to Principal Kouriki. The public library closed at five on Wednesdays, so they parked in the empty lot behind the building and walked to the school from there. A big textured biscuit of a moon lit the way.

The door to the science wing was unlocked, just as Charlie had said it would be. They slipped inside, and Blake eased the door shut behind them. Down the hall, out of sight, somebody whistled a tune in a minor key. Possibly a ghost, more likely the night janitor. Charlie led the way up the staircase to the second floor.

Ava shuddered as they stepped into classroom 211. This was now Mrs. Carr's room, no longer Mr. Trinkley's, but she felt as if she'd entered the lair of a carnivorous beast. Dim light from the hall spilled through the doorway, but most of the room was in shadow. Kylie lit half a dozen candles on Mrs. Carr's desk while Ava set up the spirit board on a student desk and arranged four chairs around it.

"Do we really need that thing?" Blake asked Ava. "Won't Mr. Trinkley just appear to us, like he did that day in physics class?"

Ava considered that. "Maybe. Maybe not. A spirit board gives us the best chance of contacting him. And if he can't speak, he can spell out messages on the board."

The four of them seated themselves around the desk. Outside, a few wispy clouds glowed silver in the moonlight. Kylie jumped when a gust of wind rattled the windows.

"Is everyone's phone off?" asked Ava.

Charlie and Kylie clicked off their phones. Blake reached for his pocket but then caught himself and sighed.

"Let's do this," said Ava.

They placed their fingertips on the spirit board's planchette. Ava spoke in a soft, singsong voice. "We come here tonight to summon the spirit of Mr. Larry Trinkley. Please, Mr. Trinkley, make your presence known."

The room was very still. No one moved or coughed

or even breathed, at least not audibly, though Ava swore she could hear hearts thumping. She sensed the conflicted feelings of her friends. They wanted Mr. Trinkley to show up, but at the same time they didn't. She felt the same way. This was scary! She hoped the group's ambivalence wouldn't interfere with their ability to connect with the spirit world.

She gave it another minute and then said, a little louder, "Mr. Larry Trinkley, are you here with us? If so, please point to *yes* on the spirit board."

Four pairs of eyes drifted to the planchette. A minute passed, then two minutes. When the planchette jerked, Blake inhaled sharply. Charlie said, "Sorry. My hand twitched."

Everyone sighed, the spell broken.

"Maybe he's not here anymore," said Kylie. "He might have, you know, moved on to the great beyond."

"Which in his case had better be hell," muttered Blake.

Ava wasn't about to give up. "Maybe one of the other ghosts can help. There are supposed to be a lot of them in the building."

"I've never seen one," said Blake. "Aside from Trinkley."

"I have," said Charlie.

They all looked at him.

Charlie shrugged like this was no big deal. "It was on one of those nights when I came here to get a book I'd forgotten. I saw this kid down the hall. He was floating above the floor, and I could see straight through him. When he saw me looking, he disappeared."

"I wonder why the ghosts don't appear more

often," said Kylie.

"Maybe they're shy," said Blake.

"Or maybe they only come out at certain times." Ava flexed her fingers. "Let's try something different."

They repositioned their fingers on the planchette. Ava said, "We invite any spirits who are nearby to join our circle. Please make your presence known."

For a minute, nothing happened. Then the candles on Mrs. Carr's desk flickered. A chill swept the room. "Someone's here," Ava murmured.

Kylie whimpered. "Oh God. I don't think I'm ready for this!"

Charlie, facing the rear of the classroom, gasped. Ava whipped her head around and saw a transparent figure floating toward them, a teenage boy who glowed as if lit from within.

"That's the same kid I saw in the hall that night," Charlie whispered.

The boy wafted to the front of the classroom and hovered above Mrs. Carr's desk. He gave the spirit board a disdainful glance. "You can take your fingers off that thing. I'm no good at spelling. Let's just talk, shall we?"

For a minute, the four of them could only gawk, their mouths hanging open. They'd summoned an actual ghost! Charlie was the first to snap out of his stupor. He scooched his chair around so he was facing the kid. "I know you. I saw you last month in the hall by the music wing."

The kid nodded. He had short brown hair and a thin face bracketed by protruding ears. He wore black-framed glasses along with a short-sleeved button-down shirt, gray trousers, and black dress shoes. "I saw you, too. I'm Robert."

"Nice to meet you, Robert. I'm Charlie. These are my friends Ava, Blake, and Kylie."

Robert waved away the introductions. "I know who you are. I see you every day. I watch you walk to your classes. I hear you talking with your friends."

Kylie said primly, "Well, I sure hope you haven't been going into the girls' restrooms."

"Of course not." Robert looked indignant. "I might be dead, but I'm not a perv." He sent an anxious glance around the group. "Did I use that word correctly? *Perv*? I try to keep up with teen slang, but it isn't easy. The lingo keeps changing."

"How long have you been here?" asked Blake.

"A long time. A long, long time." Robert drew his knees up and sat cross-legged, though what he sat on was thin air. "You summoned me. Here I am. What can I do for you?"

He bobbed gently in the air as Ava told him about Mr. Trinkley and the curse. When she was done, he said, "That's not groovy." Immediately, he slapped his forehead with the palm of his hand. "I meant *cool*—'that's not cool.' No, wait. How about 'that's a bummer'? Yeah, that's better." He cocked his head and frowned. "Or is it?"

Charlie chuckled indulgently, like a dad whose toddler just said the cutest thing. Ava said, "Forget the teen lingo, Robert. Talk the way you did when you were alive."

"But I might sound *cheugy*, and that would be a *big yikes*."

Ava huffed in exasperation. "Dude. Stop."

Robert wafted closer to them. "*Would you rather—*

that's a doozy of a curse. A really old one, too. I wouldn't be surprised if it started out as *Wouldst thou prefereth.*"

"Do you think you can break it?" asked Blake.

"Me?" Robert laughed. "Heavens, no. Ghost curses are tricky. Only the spirit who inflicted a curse can end it."

Kylie shivered and pulled her jacket more tightly around her. "I can't believe ghost curses are a thing. So any ghost at any time could decide to curse somebody?"

"Most don't, though," said Robert. "*I've* never cursed anyone. Ghost curses take a tremendous amount of power and a lot of preparation, especially for a complicated curse like Trinkley's. Of course, he's been here for a while. His powers have grown over the years. He's had time to plan out the curse, to make sure all the moving parts connect. And he probably got advice from older ghosts who know about curses."

"So you know him," said Ava.

"Let's just say I know *of* him."

"We tried to summon him," said Kylie. "He didn't show."

"I'm not surprised. He keeps to himself, stays invisible most of the time. I never saw him myself until a month or two ago." Robert's ghostly glow pulsed excitedly. "That was probably the day he cursed you. The day he temporarily became solid."

"I didn't know it was possible for a ghost to become solid," said Ava.

"It's possible, but it isn't easy. Manifesting yourself as an apparition takes tremendous energy. Becoming solid takes even more. You have to save up for years. Decades, even. That explains why I never saw him. He stayed invisible to conserve energy. And that was how he managed to appear to you as a flesh-and-blood man."

"He planned this for decades?" Ava shook her head in bewilderment. "I don't get it. He died before any of us were even born. Why does he have it out for us?"

"That is a question I cannot answer."

"We really need to talk to him," said Blake.

Robert snorted. "Too bad he doesn't seem to want to talk to *you*."

Ava pinned him with a thoughtful stare. "Maybe you can persuade him."

"Me?" Robert goggled at her. "Oh no. I'm not talking to that guy. He scares me."

"Robert, come on," pleaded Ava." Our friend *died*. And more people will die if you don't help us. Do you really want that on your conscience?"

"My conscience?" shouted Robert, his ghostly form seeming to swell. "I'm *dead*. Do you really think I still have a conscience?" He glared at Ava and she returned the glare, refusing to back down. After a few seconds, Robert looked away. He mumbled, "Actually, I do. I do have a conscience." In an even mumblier voice, he added, "I wish I didn't."

"So you'll help us?"

Robert untangled his legs and glided furiously back and forth in front of the whiteboard. He turned to glower at Ava. "I'll see what I can do. But I'm not making any promises."

Before she could thank him, he vanished.

The room warmed up quickly. The candles burned straight and tall, undisturbed by rogue air currents.

Blake said, "If Robert can't find Trinkley and bring him to us—"

Charlie finished. "—we're screwed."

Ava's heart assumed the weight of a brick as she thought back on *would you rather* day. She had reached for one card, and then another and another, before choosing the *disappear forever* one. Had a better fate been written on one of those other cards? Did her ghastly destiny really hinge on the luck of the draw? The hell with Mr. Zwick and what he thought of her—she should have refused to play Trinkley's game. She should have walked out of class that day.

With a poof, Robert came back. His hair was tousled, his glasses were crooked, and he had the harried look of a mouse that's been batted around by a cat. "I found him. Unfortunately, he's acting a bit *salty*, so I don't think—"

He broke off as the candle flames danced wildly. The room got so cold that everyone's breath puffed ghostly white. The air around them crackled with electricity.

And then Trinkley appeared, wafting in front of the whiteboard. As big as life, but not alive—dead. And not solid this time but transparent and glowing, like a paper lantern.

Kylie made a choking noise.

Mr. Trinkley sailed closer, eyeing each of them balefully. Ava tried not to flinch as he loomed in front of her. She'd never gazed into the eyes of a coiled serpent before but thought this was what it must be like.

It was impossible to know how long Trinkley would stay, so she needed to shake off her daze and get down to business. "Mr. Trinkley, thank you for joining us here tonight." Her voice trembled, a byproduct of fear compounded by uncontrollable shivering. The room temperature had surely dropped below freezing. "My classmates and I don't know why you cursed us, but we've come to humbly ask you to end the curse. Some of our friends have suffered terrible fates, and more will suffer if you don't—"

"Silence!" Trinkley spoke in a whispery hiss that seemed to come not from his mouth but from the very walls of the room, as if pumped through dozens of speakers.

He turned his eyes upon each of them in turn, and Ava watched her friends shrink from that malevolent gaze. Someone gulped. Someone else moaned. Trinkley's eyes were dark, billowing storm clouds, and when he spoke again, his roaring hiss shook the room like thunder.

"The sins of the fathers shall be visited upon the sons!"

Abruptly, the candles went out. At the same instant, Trinkley vanished.

A minute went by. Then Blake said, in a shaky voice, " 'The sins of the fathers'—what does that even mean?"

"I think it means no," said Charlie.

Ava caught a movement from the front of the classroom. Robert was still with them, though just barely. He was so faint, he was almost invisible. "I drained my battery tonight," he said. "I'm fading fast. Listen, don't give up hope. You need to have another séance, but the right people have to be here. Talk to Mr. Perry about the day Trinkley died. Ask him—"

And then Robert disappeared, too.

Chapter 20

Charlie

Charlie, Blake, and Ava arrived at school half an hour early the next morning, determined to talk to Mr. Perry before classes started. But when they entered Mr. P's classroom, they saw a stranger sitting at his desk, eating a fast-food breakfast sandwich. A substitute teacher. The guy didn't know why Mr. Perry was absent or when he might return. He suggested they check back the following day.

"We should talk to Hank," said Blake as they walked up the nearly deserted hallway. Mrs. Garcia, the Spanish teacher, was up ahead, dripping water from her collapsed umbrella all over the floor, but no one else was around. "He's been here forever. I bet he can tell us about the day Trinkley died."

"No," said Ava. "Robert told us to talk to Mr. Perry. Not Hank."

"Mr. Perry isn't here today. Hank is."

"So we talk to Perry tomorrow. One day won't make that much of a difference."

"It will if somebody dies."

"I don't think that'll happen. Everybody's being really careful."

"Not Lonnie's mom. She doesn't even know she's been cursed."

Charlie spoke up. "Maybe Lonnie should tell her."

"No," said Ava. "Lonnie's afraid her mom would let it slip to her dad, and then both parents would be cursed."

"Yeah, that would suck," Charlie conceded. He suppressed a yawn. He'd gotten up way too early today, and all for nothing.

"So can we go talk to Hank?" asked Blake.

"No!" said Ava.

No seemed to have become her favorite word. Charlie remembered when his youngest sister had gone through that phase. *Terrible twos*, his parents called it.

Blake stepped in front of Ava, bringing her to a halt. "Why are you so scared of Hank? Jeez, Ava. The guy doesn't bite."

"How many times have I told you: I'm not scared of him! I just think he's— Oh, forget it!" Ava veered around Blake and went flouncing up the hall.

Tensions were running high among the *would you rather* twenty-three (now down to twenty-two, Charlie amended grimly). Blake and Ava, in particular, had been sniping at each other a lot lately. Charlie tried not to take sides, but in this instance, he agreed with Ava. Hank seemed like a perfectly nice guy, and yet there was something off about him, something Charlie had never been able to put his finger on. Blake liked the guy, but he, Charlie, preferred to keep his distance, the same way you might skirt around a bull grazing peacefully in a meadow.

"Come on, let's go find Hank," said Blake.

Charlie hung back. "Actually, B, I don't think we should."

Blake gave him a scornful look. "Don't tell me

you're scared of Hank, too."

Charlie forced a smile. "Of course not. I'm just not sure we can trust him to keep this to himself. What if he tells Kouriki we were asking questions?"

"We'll ask him not to."

"No, I really think we should wait and talk to Mr. Perry, like Robert said."

"Fine," grumbled Blake. "Then we'd better hope he comes in tomorrow."

But Mr. Perry was out again on Friday. Now they would have to wait till Monday, and for all they knew, he might be absent then, too.

Meanwhile, the curse had claimed another victim. Liam Oswalt had broken out in a grotesque purple rash, a fate he'd chosen over chronic diarrhea.

But at least no one else had died, Charlie thought gratefully.

Not yet, anyway.

Chapter 21

Ava

On Friday after school, Ava and Kylie visited Paisley to drop off her homework assignments and see how she was doing. Paisley had been absent from school for the past three days. She'd told Ava that her feet were bright red and hot to the touch. They alternately burned like fire and itched like poison ivy. And the swelling was worse than ever. Soaking them in a solution of cool water and magnesium sulfate was the only thing that brought her any relief.

Ava had planned to visit Paisley by herself, but Kylie didn't think she should walk the streets of Pinedale alone. Safety in numbers, she said. It was a sensible precaution meant to thwart the curse.

Ava had come to believe that her *would you rather* fate, like Maddy's, would involve a kidnapper, because getting abducted—and subsequently either murdered or sold into bondage—was a common cause of involuntary disappearances. She'd looked it up on the internet. She figured she was most likely to get snatched while walking alone in public areas, where someone might pull her into a passing car, or chloroform her in a restroom, or poke a concealed gun into her back and threaten to shoot her if she didn't go with them.

Of course, there were other ways to disappear—driving into a lake, falling into a vat of acid, getting swallowed up by quicksand—but those scenarios seemed less likely.

With Kylie by her side, she made it to Paisley's house without disappearing. Another small victory! She imagined her would-be kidnapper watching from an alley and shaking his fist in frustration as she breezed by.

"How's it going?" Ava asked Paisley as she and Kylie settled themselves on the couch in the Boyds' family room. It was more a conversation starter than a true inquiry. Ava knew things weren't going well. Paisley had her feet planted in a metal washtub half filled with water, and she looked utterly wretched.

"Mom took me to a new doctor today." Paisley spoke in a dispirited monotone. "A podiatrist in Raleigh. But he's no better than the other doctors. None of them have any idea what's causing the swelling or how to make it stop."

"We know what's causing it," said Kylie. "Too bad you can't tell your doctors about the curse."

"That wouldn't help. You think they have special medicine for curses?" Paisley lifted her feet out of the water and glowered at them. They looked like two raw meatloaves with toes. "If we can't break the curse, I'll be like this for the rest of my life. I'll end up in a wheelchair. God, I hate this! I should have picked a different *would you rather* card. I'd take Liam's rash over this any day."

Ava wished there was something she could say that would make Paisley feel better. All she had to offer was, "I think we're getting somewhere, Pais. After we talk to Mr. Perry, we'll hold another séance, and that might do the trick. Let's hope for the best, okay?"

Paisley shrugged in a way that said she had no interest in hoping for the best. She mumbled, "Henry Schiffhauer was absent that day. Do you remember? Talk about lucky—he had strep throat." She stared wistfully into space. "I almost skipped school, too. I had cramps that morning, and I was going to stay home, but I didn't want to miss the auditions for the junior class play. So I dragged myself to school." She gave a bitter laugh. "And I didn't even get a part in the play. God. Why didn't I stay home?"

Paisley seemed determined to wallow in misery, so Ava gave up trying to lift her spirits. She and Kylie just let her vent.

"I feel so bad for her," Kylie said as the two of them left Paisley's house.

"Me too," said Ava, though privately she thought Paisley's fate was preferable to her own. Sure, Paisley's affliction was unpleasant, but at least she hadn't been wrenched away from her family.

Kylie stretched her arms out, checking for sprinkles. Rain had poured down relentlessly over the past few days, including most of the day today, but the clouds finally seemed to be thinning. Kylie slipped her umbrella into her purse.

"Come on, I'll walk you home," she said.

They cut through the middle of town. When they were across the street from Lou's Diner, Kylie stopped abruptly. "Ooh, Hank just went in the diner. Should we go ask him about Mr. Trinkley?"

Ava sucked in a sharp breath, goosebumps sprouting on her arms like they always did when Hank was close by. Maybe she *was* scared of him, just a little, though she would never admit that to Blake. She realized now that Blake was right—at this point, Hank was probably their best hope. They wouldn't be able to talk to Mr. Perry until Monday, and not even then if he was still absent. Meanwhile, the clock was ticking, people were suffering, and more deaths would occur if the curse didn't end soon. Ava herself awoke with a gasp each morning, wondering if today would be the day she disappeared.

Maybe it was time to cast her fears aside and talk to Hank.

"Let's do it," she said, stepping into the street before she could lose her nerve.

But as she took that first step, a circular darkness opened up at her feet, dense as a black hole in outer space. A steady rushing noise roared from its depths. Time seemed to slow down, and from a great distance she heard Kylie screech, "Ava, watch out!"

Ava couldn't halt the momentum of her stride. She was just starting to step down, down into that void when someone grabbed her arm and yanked her back.

"What is wrong with you, girl?" bellowed a deep voice. "Christ almighty! You need to watch where you're going."

Ava looked up into the furious face of a hard-hatted worker, a guy around her dad's age. "Didn't you see the cones?" the man asked incredulously.

Ava blinked. What cones? She wasn't sure what had just happened. She glanced around, and then she saw them: several orange traffic cones surrounding a large, round hole at the side of the street. A sewer access hole. The metal cover lay nearby.

The worker released Ava's arm but continued his rebuke. "You need to be more careful. If you'd fallen in, we wouldn't have been able to save you. With all the rain we've had lately, the storm sewers are gushing. You'd have been swept into the river and from there to the next river and the next until you ended up in the ocean. Odds are, your body never would have been recovered."

Ava stared at him in slack-mouthed horror. She whispered, "I would have disappeared forever."

The man nodded grimly. "Watch where you're going next time, okay?"

Ava followed Kylie up the sidewalk and collapsed onto a rain-soaked bench, limp with shock. Apparently, she could disappear forever even with someone by her side.

Her gaze moved from the orange traffic cones to the ominous hole in the street to the workers milling around in their fluorescent green vests. How had she missed all that activity? She must have been so anxious about approaching Hank that it had slipped past her awareness.

"Holy crap," said Kylie, plopping down next to her. "The curse almost got you, Ava."

That made it sound like the curse was a sentient being, a cunning enemy. This wasn't the first time Ava had thought of it that way. Nonetheless, she shuddered.

"But you know," Kylie went on, "this might be a good thing."

Ava looked at her blankly.

"Maybe you beat the curse. Maybe it only gets one chance to do you in. It tried to get you, but it failed, so maybe that's the end of it. For you, anyway."

Ava could only hope. And if Kylie's theory wasn't correct—well, maybe the curse would at least leave her alone for a while. Out of humiliation or respect or something.

Once Ava and Kylie had calmed down, they entered the diner to look for Hank. He was nowhere to be seen.

Chapter 22

Charlie

On Saturday morning, Charlie was restless. His sisters were spending the day with their grandparents, so at least he wasn't stuck babysitting. He started to play the latest game V-Play had sent for testing, but couldn't concentrate. On a whim, he opened a search engine on his computer and typed Mr. Perry's full name and *Pinedale NC* into the search window. Like magic, Mr. P's address came up: 514 Goldfinch Lane. That was on the Bodega side of town.

After lunch, Charlie clicked his phone on and typed a text message to Blake. Then he remembered Blake no longer had a cell phone, so he had to run across the street to Blake's house like a kid from the 1960s. Blake himself opened the door. Charlie presented his plan, and Blake said he was down with it.

Charlie sent Ava a text: —*got mr p's address u wanna go see him with blake & me?*—

He and Blake discussed the situation while they waited for Ava to respond.

"That 'sins of the fathers' shit has me freaked out," said Blake. "It sounds like Trinkley is punishing us for something our fathers did. But my dad was a good man, a military hero. I doubt he ever did anything bad in his whole life. Plus, he wasn't even from around here. He grew up in Pennsylvania. He never met Trinkley."

"Same with my dad," said Charlie. "Except he's from Oklahoma and never served in the military."

"Twenty-three students got cursed. How could Trinkley have it out for all of us?"

"It's not all of us, though. Some people got two good options," Charlie reminded him.

"Yeah, but only a few. And it wasn't like he forced our card on us. We were free to choose. I could just as easily have picked a good card. You could have picked a bad one."

Charlie sighed. None of this made sense.

He checked his phone, but Ava hadn't responded. He thought she had dance lessons or kick-boxing or something on Saturdays, though he was pretty sure that was in the morning.

"I hope Ava's doing okay," he said. "That was some scary shit she went through yesterday."

Blake looked at him sharply. "What are you talking about? What scary shit?"

"You know—the sewer thing. How she almost fell in."

Blake's eyes seemed to darken.

"What, she didn't tell you?"

"No," said Blake. "She didn't."

Well, this was awkward. "I'm sorry, man. Look, it's hard to keep in touch with someone who doesn't have a phone. I'm sure she'll tell you all about it next time she sees you."

"Right," said Blake. But his jaw twitched like he was clenching it.

Charlie wished Blake and Ava would sort out their differences. Life was stressful enough without the prickliness that had sprung up between them.

He sent Ava another text, giving her Mr. P's address and inviting her to meet him and Blake there. If she couldn't make it, no worries. He and Blake would handle the meeting without her.

Mr. Perry lived in a yellow ranch house surrounded by a small, tidy yard. A bald tree stood to the left of the walkway. Charlie was good at identifying trees by their leaves, but he couldn't tell what kind this one was because someone had done a thorough job of raking up the fallen leaves.

Mr. Perry answered the door. He wore a faded flannel shirt and gray sweatpants, an outfit Charlie suspected was the Mr. P version of pajamas.

"Well, well. If it isn't Charlie Washington and Blake Pedley from school. To what do I owe this great pleasure?"

"You're sick?" asked Blake, and belatedly Charlie noticed Mr. Perry's red nose.

Mr. Perry sniffled. "I caught a cold a couple of days back. I'm getting better, though. I expect to be back at school on Monday." He glanced from Charlie to Blake. "Do you boys need something? Or are you just missing your favorite teacher?"

"Can we come in and talk to you?" asked Charlie.

Mr. Perry pushed the screen door open. "Enter at your own risk. The place is probably teeming with germs."

Charlie and Blake stepped into Mr. P's living room. Mr. Perry motioned them toward a brown plaid sofa and then disappeared down a hallway.

Charlie looked around the tiny room. There wasn't much in it furniture-wise: the sofa, an easy chair, a coffee table, a floor lamp, and a boxy TV. A painting of a lake at sunset hung on the wall above the sofa. Everything looked worn and outdated, like family heirlooms passed down through the generations. But the room was as clean and tidy as the yard.

A text message pinged to life on Charlie's phone. He pulled the phone out of his pocket, expecting to see Ava's name, but it turned out to be his mom telling him to stop at the store to get milk on his way home. Story of his life. It seemed like every time he went out, he got tasked with running a household errand.

Mr. Perry came back with two glasses of water and a bowl of pretzels. "I haven't been to the grocery store for a while. This is the best I can offer." He set the snacks on the coffee table and sat in the easy chair.

"No, this is great. Thanks, Mr. Perry." Charlie snatched a pretzel out of the bowl and bit in. He tried not to grimace when he realized it was stale.

"What we want to talk to you about," said Blake, "is Mr. Trinkley."

"The substitute teacher you asked me about at the funeral home? I told you, I don't know the man."

"It's actually the other Mr. Trinkley we're interested in. The one who taught math at the school years ago."

"Larry Trinkley," said Charlie.

Mr. Perry's gaze bounced back and forth between the two of them. "Now why on Earth would you be interested in him?"

Charlie had expected this question. He'd even formulated an answer: *We're doing a project on the history of the school.* But looking into Mr. P's intelligent blue eyes, he realized he couldn't lie to the man. Mr. P deserved the truth. Well—maybe not the whole truth, but at least a portion of it.

"We can't tell you that," he said. "All I can say is that it's very important that we find out everything we can about Mr. Trinkley. It's literally a matter of life and death."

Mr. Perry sucked his cheeks in as he thought that over. "What do you want to know?"

Chapter 23

Maddy

When the ceiling creaked in a certain spot, Maddy knew Tommy was coming. Old boards were like arthritic old bones, and the creaking from above told her the house was quite elderly. She heard the metallic slide of the deadbolt, and then the cellar door opened. Her throat tightened as Tommy came down the stairs carrying her lunch tray.

"Mac and cheese, your favorite," he said, though the two of them had never discussed her favorite foods.

Seeing him with his hands full, she thought about giving him a hard shove and running for the stairs. It wasn't the first time she'd had that thought. But there was always a gun handle poking out of his pocket, and she knew she couldn't outrace a bullet.

Tommy sat across the table from her while she ate, talking nonstop in a mumbly monotone. Reminiscing, mostly. The guy was fixated on high school. There'd been a class bully who used to pound on him, but the kid had eventually been expelled. Several teachers hadn't liked him and had given him bad grades. But mostly he talked about a girl named Rachel. Her shining brown hair, her bright blue eyes. The mesmerizing sparkle of her golden hoop earrings. The interesting part was that whenever he talked about

Rachel, he always said *you,* not *she.*

So that was it, then. Her kidnapper thought she was his long-lost love. That struck her as a tired trope, one she'd seen on countless crime shows on TV. She felt vaguely disappointed that this thing, whatever it was—a curse, a jinx, a malicious deity toying with her—hadn't managed to come up with a more original plotline.

"Oh," said Tommy, interrupting himself halfway through a lengthy reminiscence. "You'll never guess what I saw today." He didn't give her a chance to guess, not that she would have been able to. "I saw someone walking one of those dogs you like so much. You know the kind I mean."

"Oh yes!" she said. "I love that kind of dog."

"What are they called again? I can't think of the name."

She frowned into the air. "Neither can I."

"I think—I think it starts with a *p.*"

Poodle? Pomeranian? She almost took a wild guess, but then Tommy smacked a hand on the table and said, "Pekinese! That's it."

"Yes! Pekinese. They're so adorable. I've always wanted one." Not! Maddy Eppley was more of a cat person.

"Well, maybe I'll get you one," Tommy said.

"That would be amazing. Yeah, we should get a dog. I can take care of it while you're at work."

Because if they had a joint pet, he wouldn't kill her...would he?

She glanced at his face and saw that frown, saw how his eyes had clouded over like a storm blown in from an unexpected direction, and she really, really did not like that look, so she laid a hand on his arm and said, "Hey, what's in the bag? Did you bring me a present?" She'd seen a small gift bag dangling from his hand when he'd come down the stairs.

Tommy blinked several times, and she watched his face return to normal. "Yeah," he said. "Yeah, I did. I brought you a present."

He reached down and came up holding the gift bag, which he placed on the table. "Go ahead. Open it."

"Ooh. I wonder what it is." Maddy tried to look excited.

Tommy moved his chair to her side of the table, so close that his thigh touched hers. The scent of fabric softener wafted up her nose. It was a clean, pleasant scent but one that nauseated her, because he was way too close. She scooted to the edge of her seat, trying to get away.

She reached into the bag and pulled out a DVD, the first movie in that old vampire franchise.

"Oh!" she said. "I love this movie." That was true enough. She'd seen the entire series several times.

Tommy smiled shyly. "Remember when I took you to see it? Remember how much you liked it? Now we can watch it again. We'll finally have our second date—and I bet it'll be even better than the first."

He moved his face toward hers, his lips beginning to pucker, his eyelids drifting closed.

"No!" shrieked Maddy, suddenly realizing that she'd played along too well. She was sure she was about to be raped, though he wouldn't see it that way. He would think he was making love to Rachel because this guy was crazy, wacko, bonkers, and all she could think to do in the moment was try to shatter his delusions.

She jumped up and backed away from the table. "I'm not Rachel—I'm Maddy!" Her voice shrilled, rattling her own eardrums. "My name is Madeline Mae Eppley, and I want to go home. I want my mom! I miss my family and my friends, and I know they miss me, so please, please, let me go! Just let me go!" She was crying hard by the time she got to the end of the rant.

She cowered against the wall, gasping and snuffling, as Tommy got to his feet. He shot her a menacing look and said, "You're just like all the others." Then he stomped up the stairs, leaving her dinner tray behind.

He didn't even empty her poop bucket.

Chapter 24

Blake

"What do you want to know?" asked Mr. Perry

Charlie said, "Whatever you can tell us about the day Mr. Trinkley died."

"The day he died. You want to know about the day Larry died. That was a long time ago. A mighty long time. I don't know if I can remember much." Mr. Perry plucked a tissue from a box on the coffee table and blew his nose noisily.

"Please," said Blake. "Like Charlie said, it's really important."

He sipped his water, more out of politeness than of thirst. He tasted chlorine, which told him Mr. Perry had filled the glasses at the kitchen sink. Blake's mom would not have approved. Being a medical professional, she often lectured him and his brother about the dangers of chlorinated drinking water. She bought only chlorine-free bottled water for her family.

"Okay," Mr. Perry said in a grim, quiet voice. "I'll tell you what I can." But before he could begin, he was besieged by a series of wet, phlegmy coughs. Blake imagined germs rushing across the room like a fleet of microscopic doomsday missiles. He flattened himself against the back of the sofa, trying to get out of range.

"Sorry," said Mr. Perry. He grabbed an aerosol can

of disinfectant from the coffee table and sprayed the air. Blake's head was engulfed in a chemical cloud, and he wondered if breathing it was better or worse for him than inhaling cold germs. Or drinking chlorinated water.

He'd never imagined Mr. Perry's house would be so fraught with peril.

"I saw Larry leave the school that afternoon," Mr. Perry said. "I remember because I thought it was odd that he left through a back door instead of going out front, where his car was parked. I watched through a window as he walked toward the woods. Of course, I didn't know he was headed for Bugbane Rock. I just thought he wanted to get a little fresh air and exercise before he went home."

"He was alone when he left?" asked Charlie.

"Yes, alone. I saw him pull something out of his shirt pocket. A slip of paper. He looked at it and then put it back." Mr. Perry shrugged. "Maybe it was a grocery list, something unimportant. It wasn't mentioned in the news reports."

"Any ideas about why he would have gone to Bugbane Rock?" asked Blake.

"Ideas? Sure. But they're just that—ideas. Fanciful thinking, perhaps. I'm not sure I feel comfortable sharing them."

"We won't tell anyone," said Charlie. "We promise."

"Please?" Blake leaned forward. "It could really help us."

Mr. Perry must have seen the desperation in their eyes. He nodded reluctantly.

"As I told you before, Larry wasn't well-liked by

his students. And the feeling was mutual. The kids constantly pulled pranks on him. They'd soap his car windows, draw dirty pictures on his blackboard. Once somebody set a live squirrel loose in his classroom. Another time somebody did number two in his wastebasket. He usually managed to find out who the perpetrators were, and he made sure they got punished. Which prompted them to pull an even nastier prank to get even. Which made Larry even madder. It was quite the vicious circle."

He fell silent, staring morosely out the front window. Blake, trying to keep the momentum of the conversation going, said, "Are you saying Mr. Trinkley's accident wasn't really an accident? Do you think some of those students got back at him by killing him?"

"No! I never said that. Don't put words in my mouth, boy. I just think some of those kids knew something. Maybe they were there when the accident happened. Maybe they even lured Larry to Bugbane Rock. There was one particular group that really had it out for him. Shane, Corey, Duncan, and Laura. They were constantly thinking up new ways to torment him."

Blake felt Charlie tense up beside him. "Duncan? You don't mean Duncan Nolty, do you? Deej's dad?"

Mr. Perry's mouth tightened. "That's the one."

"Laura," said Blake. "That's Maddy's mom's name."

"Yes," said Mr. Perry, "it is."

Wow, thought Blake. So two of the students who'd played *would you rather* had parents who'd clashed with Mr. Trinkley twenty years earlier.

The sins of the fathers…

He asked, "What makes you think those kids might've been at Bugbane Rock?"

"Just a hunch. For starters, I saw them in the building that day, after hours. They said they'd stayed to attend the girls' volleyball game in the gym, but that struck me as odd. Those four rarely attended school sporting events."

He paused to blow his nose again. "But that wasn't the only thing. Those kids were never the same after Larry's death. They'd always been rambunctious, arrogant, devil-may-care. After that day they were subdued. Anxious, even. And they all became self-destructive in one way or another. Duncan started drinking. Laura slept with any guy who smiled at her. As for Shane, he decided to go car-surfing one day and died doing it. Twenty years old and his life was over."

"What about the fourth kid?" asked Charlie. "Corey?"

"Died of a drug overdose in his early twenties."

Blake and Charlie took a minute to digest those grim facts.

"The newspaper article says two hikers found Mr. Trinkley's body," said Blake. "Did they see anybody?"

"Not to my knowledge. Of course, they didn't show up till later in the afternoon. If anybody was there when Larry fell, they were long gone by the time the hikers arrived."

Charlie's phone pinged. He pulled it out of his jacket pocket and took a look. "It's Ava."

"Oh, good," said Blake. "Tell her not to bother—"

"No, wait." Charlie frowned down at his phone. "It's not Ava. It's her mom on Ava's phone."

Out of nowhere, a cannonball slammed into

Blake's chest. He watched Charlie's mouth drop open as he read the text. He saw the horror dulling Charlie's eyes as Charlie turned to face him, and he didn't want to hear what Charlie was about to say, did not want to hear it, la-la-la, and yet he was frozen, unable to do anything but sit and wait for those unthinkable words to strike his eardrums.

"Ava's gone missing!"

Chapter 25

Tommy

He should have known the girl wasn't Rachel. The problem—with this girl, and with the others before her—was that he tended to focus on similarities and ignore differences. He couldn't help it. He wanted Rachel back so badly that wishful thinking often eclipsed objectivity.

This one's name was Madeline—Maddy for short. Tommy had been passing through the small town of Pinedale and, on a whim, had stopped off at a diner. That was where he'd first seen her. She'd been talking to her mother, the server named Laura, who had just brought Tommy a big, steaming square of lasagna. Tommy's breath had stuck in his throat along with a chunk of lasagna noodle because there was Rachel standing not eight feet away. Her back was to him, but he recognized her immediately because he knew her from every angle. That shining brown hair, that slender frame, the coltish legs. He couldn't tear his gaze away.

When she turned, he saw that the eyes were different—Rachel's were bright blue, whereas this girl's were brown—but that could be explained away by contact lenses. Tommy wasn't troubled by it. Those eyes sparked with the same zest for life.

A hot shiver went through him. He'd found her.

His long-lost Rachel.

He often thought back on that day in life skills class when Rachel had entered his world. While most teachers used alphabetical order for their seating arrangements, Mr. Brehm didn't care where people sat. Tommy had ended up at the desk next to Rachel's, which meant he could study her profile from the corner of his eye while she listened to Brehm's droning lecture.

Rachel was a new student, having moved from Missouri with her parents over the summer. Tommy was instantly smitten, though he was too terrified to speak to her. Two weeks went by with nothing but furtive, longing glances on Tommy's part. And then one day Rachel turned those dazzling blue eyes on him and asked if he had a pencil she could borrow. Tommy gave her a pencil and told her to keep it, even though it was his only one and he had to go to the school office after class to ask for a new one. And that was that. The ice was broken. The story of Tommy and Rachel had begun.

They chatted every afternoon before class started. Thankfully, Mr. Brehm was usually late. He had lunch immediately prior to fifth period and tended to linger in the teacher's lounge long past the ringing of the bell. The students definitely weren't getting their money's worth as far as life skills instruction went, but Tommy wasn't complaining.

He finally worked up the nerve to ask Rachel out on a date. And she said yes! She suggested that they go see that vampire movie, which really wasn't his cup of tea, but he agreed, feigning enthusiasm. She'd been talking about that movie for a while, actually. She really wanted to see it but had no one to go with, and that was what had prompted Tommy to ask her out in the first place.

After the movie, he drove her home, and it was such a nice night, star-spangled and unseasonably balmy, that they went for a walk. Rachel lived in a semi-rural area, and the houses were spaced pretty far apart. The people down the road had a dog, a Pekinese that yipped incessantly as Tommy and Rachel passed by.

"Hi, Muffin. Hey, boy," Rachel said in a high-pitched baby-talk voice, and then she told Tommy how awful she thought it was that the owners kept Muffin tied up in their yard. He had a cute little doghouse to shelter him from the elements, but still. Why have a dog if you weren't going to bring him into the house and interact with him?

"I wish I had a dog like Muffin," Rachel said. "I love Pekinese."

"Maybe I'll get you one," said Tommy, only half-joking.

Rachel laughed and explained that dog ownership at this point in her life was out of the question because her parents had put their collective foot down. Dogs were smelly and noisy and entirely too much work. Rachel had promised to do it all—the feeding, the walking, the poop cleanup—but her mom had pointed out that she would be going off to college in less than a year, and who would be stuck taking care of the hypothetical pooch then?

"A stuffed dog, though. That would be fine," said Rachel, giving Tommy a sidelong glance.

He hatched his plan immediately. He had an uncle

who did taxidermy on the side, a tradecraft Tommy found fascinating. The uncle did mostly wildlife mounts—foxes, pheasants, deer heads for hunters—but Tommy knew that any animal could be taxidermied.

He told Uncle Ned there was this girl he liked, and her dog was terminally ill, and she wanted to preserve him in a form she could keep forever. He, Tommy, would pay whatever it cost. Uncle Ned had smiled and said *ah, young love*, and hadn't made Tommy pay a thing. He'd even put a rush on it, not that the taxidermy process could be rushed. It could take up to a year, depending on the size of the animal. But since a Pekinese was small, this job should take only a few months. That was longer than Tommy had bargained for, but what could he do? He would have to be patient.

When Rachel told him Muffin had gone missing, Tommy said that was a good thing because it meant he'd escaped his crappy life. He was probably in a better place.

They never did have a second date. Rachel suddenly got busy. She'd started to make friends and had signed up for horseback-riding lessons and always seemed to have more homework than Tommy had. The two of them still chatted in life skills class, but since it was a half-year elective, the course ended shortly before Christmas. The only other classes they had together were English and civics, but Tommy didn't sit near Rachel. When she saw him in the halls, she would flash a vague smile, though she never stopped to talk. When Jake Guthrie was at her side, she ignored him completely.

He kept hounding Uncle Ned. Almost done? Next week, maybe? The dog, he was sure, would fix everything. Rachel would be so touched by his thoughtfulness that things would go back to the way they'd been in life skills class, and he would finally get that second date.

At last the job was finished. Tommy wrapped the box up in fancy paper and took it to Rachel's house early one Saturday evening. Rachel's mouth formed a surprised O when she answered the door. She said that unfortunately she didn't have time to visit with him because she was getting ready to go out. Tommy assured her this would only take a few minutes.

Rachel was home alone because her parents had gone out to dinner with her dad's work associates. Tommy handed her the box and said, "This is for you," and Rachel asked, "Why?"

Tommy said, "Because I want to make you happy."

She stared at the present for a long time—warily, like she thought a bomb might be inside. Finally, she tore off the wrapping paper. She lifted the lid off the box. She looked down at Muffin. And then she screamed.

For a fraction of a second Tommy thought it was a scream of joy. Then he realized it wasn't.

"Oh my God. Oh my God, is that—" She backed away, shaking her head. "No, no, you didn't. Tell me you didn't—"

Tommy stared at her, perplexed. "You said—you said you wanted a dog like Muffin."

"*Like* Muffin," she shrilled. "Not Muffin himself! Not *dead* Muffin."

"You talked about a stuffed dog. You said—"

"A *stuffed animal*! The kind you get at a toy store!"

Tommy said, "Oh."

"You murdered him? You murdered my neighbors' dog? I—I can't believe this!"

When she put it like that—

It occurred to Tommy that he might be in trouble with Muffin's owners.

The screaming resumed. Rachel called him the most awful names, including *freak*, which his father used to call him before he'd died, and sometimes afterward, too. She wouldn't stop screaming, and he had to make her stop, he had to, because the screaming was slicing through his head like a meat cleaver, and then… and then…

He could never remember what happened after that.

Now he had a girl in his cellar who wasn't Rachel, which meant Rachel was still out there. He would have to keep searching. Meanwhile, he needed to get rid of this girl. This girl called Madeline.

Chapter 26

Charlie

"We need to hold another séance," Charlie said as he and Blake got into the car outside Mr. Perry's house. "It's our only chance to save Ava and Maddy. But remember what Robert said before he disappeared? The right people have to be there."

"Deej's dad," said Blake. "Maddy's mom."

"Yep."

"But we don't even know if they were at Bugbane Rock that day."

"Doesn't matter. They tormented him. Maybe that made him mad enough to do the curse."

Charlie unzipped his jacket and put his window down. Although the November air was cool, the unfiltered sunshine had heated the car up like a greenhouse.

"It's not fair," said Blake. "Maddy and Deej aren't the ones who tormented Mr. Trinkley. Their parents are."

"Yeah, but when the kids who tormented him were still in school, he probably wasn't powerful enough to curse them. Remember what Robert said about saving up energy over the years? By the time he'd gained enough power, those kids were grown up and gone."

"Sins of the fathers," Blake mused. "But why

punish the rest of us? We never even met the guy till that day in Zwick's class."

"I don't think he cares who he hurts. He just wants to hurt people. I figure he's like a school shooter who enters the building and starts blowing random people away. Hopefully, once Deej's dad and Maddy's mom apologize, he'll end the curse. I think that's what Robert was getting at."

"But if we invite them to the séance, we'll have to tell them about the curse. That'll put their lives in danger."

"Do you really think they'll care? Their kids are dead. Well, Deej for sure. Maddy probably."

"And Ava possibly."

Charlie's shoulders sagged. "Yeah. Ava."

"Where is she, C? What could have happened to her?" Blake sounded like he was on the verge of tears.

Charlie didn't have an answer. He didn't even have a guess.

Ava's mom had called Charlie after that first devastating text message. She'd been out running errands earlier in the day. She and Ava had planned to visit Ava's grandparents in the afternoon, but when she got home, Ava wasn't there. When she called Ava's cell phone, she heard it ringing in another room. That told her something was wrong, because Ava never went anywhere without her phone. Now the whole family was out searching for her, including grandparents, aunts, uncles, and cousins. Their efforts, Charlie knew, would be futile. Ava wouldn't be found unless the curse ended—and maybe not even then.

"So let's say we get Trinkley to end the curse," Blake said. "That should mean Ava and Maddy turn up.

It should mean I get my cell phone back. Right?"

"In theory," said Charlie. "It all depends on the algorithm."

"Algorithm?" Blake raised one eyebrow. "Dude, it's a curse, not a computer program."

"Yeah, yeah. I just mean there's probably a set of rules that govern the curse. You know, like, how soon it goes into effect, the time frame for when each individual curse comes true, and whether everything goes back to normal once the curse ends."

Outside the car, somebody called, "Ava! Ava!" in a desperate, high-pitched voice. Charlie glanced out his window and saw one of Ava's cousins trotting down the sidewalk.

"Let's assume the best-case scenario," said Blake. "The curse ends, Ava and Maddy turn up, I get my phone back, et cetera, et cetera. What about Deej? Does he come back to life?"

Charlie sucked a breath in through his teeth. "I don't know, B. Death seems like a hard thing to come back from."

They sat in glum silence for a minute.

"We should get over to Mr. Nolty's house," said Charlie, putting the car in gear. "Deej used to complain about how his dad liked to go out drinking in Raleigh on Saturday nights. I don't know if he still does that, but if he does, we need to catch him before he leaves."

It took four doorbell rings and three minutes of waiting on the porch before Mr. Nolty came to the door. He looked awful, his eyes bleary, his skin sallow. Smelled bad, too, a combination of sour whiskey and stale sweat.

He didn't say a word but simply swung the door

wide open. They followed him into the living room. The house looked like a garbage dump and smelled like one, too. Several empty booze bottles lay on the living room floor. A bottle of whiskey, half full, sat on the coffee table, balanced precariously on the edge of a thick coaster. Also on the coffee table were several plates of congealed food. It looked like Mr. Nolty had tried to eat but couldn't manage more than a few bites.

Deej's dad dropped into a recliner and slouched there, his eyes unfocused. Charlie moved a laundry basket of wrinkled clothes from the couch to the floor so he and Blake could sit down. He heard the Noltys' old hound dog, Beast, baying in the backyard: *ah-roo-roo-roo.* He hoped Beast wasn't slowly starving to death now that Deej wasn't around to feed him.

For the longest time, nobody spoke. Charlie felt tongue-tied in the face of Mr. Nolty's grief. What could he say to a man who had just lost his only child?

"How—how are you holding up?" he finally asked, because that was something he'd heard his mother say to bereaved people. But it was a dumb question. Charlie guessed that nobody held up well after the loss of a loved one, and Mr. Nolty seemed to be doing worse than most, judging by his dead-eyed stare and the filthiness of the house.

Deej's dad spoke so softly that Charlie could barely hear him. "You never expect your kid to die before you do. It all went by so quick. He was born, he grew up, and boom! Just like that, he's gone."

"We're so sorry," said Blake. "Deej was our good friend. We miss him so much."

Mr. Nolty's mouth cycled through a series of contortions, and Charlie could tell he was fighting a full-blown meltdown. When he spoke again, his voice trembled. "He was the best son. God knows he parented me better than I did him. Why, I remember how he used to…" And he launched into a lengthy Deej story.

Charlie listened with one ear while trying to figure out how to steer the conversation from grief therapy to *we want you to risk your life to help us.* It turned out he didn't have to worry about that, because when Mr. Nolty paused to swig whiskey from the bottle, Blake jumped in and got right to the point.

"Mr. Nolty, we know this is a hard time for you, but we really need your help."

Blake told him about Mr. Trinkley and the curse. As he talked, a range of emotions flitted across Mr. Nolty's face: disbelief, horror, anger, guilt.

After Blake finished, Mr. Nolty was quiet for a long time, the bottle of whiskey propped between his legs like a small, docile pet. Finally he said, in a voice so heavy it practically dragged on the ground, "I never told anybody what happened that day. Maybe it's time I did."

Chapter 27

Duncan Nolty, Sr. (twenty years earlier)

The second week of school was turning out to be even worse than the first, thanks to the D-plus Duncan had scored on the math review quiz. What a hateful, arrogant, unfair a-hole Mr. Trinkley was. Did he really expect people to remember how to solve equations? Everyone knew the teenage brain atrophied over the summer, and last week's review sessions hadn't been enough to get Duncan's math mind back into gear.

Of course, Duncan's D-plus wasn't as bad as Shane's F. Shane was livid and swore he would get back at Trinkley with his best prank yet. Or worst, depending on how you looked at it. Duncan couldn't imagine how Shane would top his premier prank from last year: taking a dump in Trinkley's wastebasket. That was a whodunnit Trinkley had never solved, though he might have had his suspicions. Shane wasn't the only person who'd pranked Trinkley, but he was the most creative.

Of the four of them in their little group—Shane, Duncan, Laura, and Corey—Shane was the only one who'd had to go to summer school. His final math grade last year had been a D-minus, a smidge below a passing grade. He'd done extra-credit work to get himself up to a solid D, but Mr. Trinkley said it wasn't enough. Shane had expressed his wrath through the wastebasket dump.

As for Duncan, he'd squeaked by with a C-minus, which was fine by him but had dismayed his parents. They worried about things like getting into colleges, though that made no sense to Duncan. The plans were already laid. Duncan would eventually join his father and uncle at the family landscaping business, so who cared if he did or didn't get into a good college—or if he skipped college altogether? It wasn't like his family would refuse to hire him.

Math had always been his worst subject. He'd hoped to get the new teacher, Ms. Glotfelty, because he'd heard she was a good instructor and an easy grader, but he'd ended up in Trinkley's class again. Judging by that review quiz, which Trinkley had sprung on them two days ago, it looked like this year would be a repeat of last year.

Shane elbowed Duncan as they walked up the hall to math class. "Look at them, Dunc. I'm telling you, he wants to jump her bones."

Mr. Trinkley and Ms. Glotfelty were next-door neighbors in the math wing. Between classes, they usually stood in the hall chatting while they waited for their classrooms to fill up. That was the only time Mr. Trinkley's a-holery seemed to subside. When Ms. Glotfelty was around, he smiled. His posture softened. His voice lost that prickly quality. And sometimes, when Mr. Trinkley listened to her speak, Duncan saw his mouth tremble. Shane was probably right. Mr. Trinkley had the hots for the new math teacher.

Ms. Glotfelty had come to the school last year after Christmas to fill in for Mrs. Dunmeyer, who'd gone on maternity leave. But Mrs. Dunmeyer had eventually decided to stay home and be a full-time mom, so the school had hired Ms. Glotfelty permanently.

Trinkley had probably done a happy dance when he'd found out about that.

Duncan had a feeling Shane was hatching a plan for payback that would somehow involve Ms. Glotfelty. That very day at lunchtime, Shane unveiled his scheme.

"We'll put a note on his desk, signed with Ms. Glotfelty's name. The note will say she has feelings for him and wants to meet somewhere so they can talk. I'm thinking Bugbane Rock. Trinkley will hike up there, and he'll feel like an idiot when she doesn't show. It'll be gnarly!"

"Why Bugbane Rock?" asked Corey. "Wouldn't it make more sense for her to invite him over to her classroom?"

"Bugbane Rock is more romantic. If he goes up there, it'll prove he likes her, and we can milk that in the future. Plus, we can hide in that cave near the top of the cliff and watch the fun."

"I'll write the note," said Laura. "I think I can imitate Ms. Glotfelty's handwriting."

Mr. Trinkley always stayed after school to prepare the following day's lesson. When he left his classroom for a restroom break, Duncan placed Laura's note on his desk. Then the four of them headed for the back door.

The humid air engulfed Duncan as he exited the building. He felt as if he'd stepped into the mouth of a gargantuan warm-blooded creature. The sun glimmered behind a thin layer of clouds, opaque as a congealed egg yolk, but he still felt its heat. And the woods weren't any cooler. The lush September foliage hung limp and bedraggled.

He tried to enjoy the hike even though he felt a little bit bad about what they were doing to Trinkley. When it came to girls and romance, Duncan's hopes had been dashed plenty of times. He couldn't help but empathize. Still, that didn't mean he was opposed to their plan. Trinkley was a jerk and deserved every bad thing that happened to him.

They reached a V-shaped fork in the trail. The main path continued to the right, while a narrower path to the left sloped steeply upward. They veered left and hiked up to the rocky cliff. The last few yards were hairy—they had to shuffle along a narrow ledge—but they made it safely to the cave. From there they had an unobstructed view of the flat rocks below and the creek beyond.

Ten minutes passed. Duncan's heart flopped when he spotted a flash of color below, but it turned out to be random hikers, a guy and a girl, who spent a minute smooching on the flat rocks at the creek's edge before continuing on their way.

A few minutes later, they heard someone else coming. Shane poked his head out of the cave and hissed, "It's him!"

Mr. Trinkley strutted into view. He stepped onto a big flat rock and stood there with his hands on his hips, staring into the burbling creek. Trying to act nonchalant, thought Duncan, though the way he shifted from foot to foot said he was anything but.

They let a few minutes go by. Trinkley glanced at his watch. He peered down the path. He paced back and forth on the rock.

A malicious grin sprouted on Shane's face. He called, in a falsetto voice, "Ooh, Ms. Glotfelty, I luhhhvvv you."

Trinkley whirled toward the cliff. Duncan, peeking out from the cave, watched his expression change from bewilderment to fury. "Who said that? Who's up there?"

Shane continued, "May I nibble your neck, Ms. Glotfelty?"

Laura giggled.

Duncan had to get in on this. He chirped, "You're the girl of my dreams, Ms. Glotfelty. I think about you every night when I put my hand down my jammy pants!"

That cracked everyone up. Everyone except Trinkley.

"You little bastards!" he roared. "I'll have you expelled, every last one of you."

"Too bad you don't know who we are," Shane taunted in that high-pitched voice.

"But I soon will," shouted Trinkley. "By God, I will."

And he started to scale the cliff.

"Whoa," said Laura. They hadn't anticipated this.

There was no way they could get off the cliff without being seen by Trinkley. And if he made it to the cave, he would certainly catch them, because there was nowhere to hide. The cave was shallow, little more than a sizable dent in the face of the cliff.

They were screwed.

They shrank against the rear wall of the cave. They heard Trinkley's breath rasping as he got closer. "Shit!" whimpered Shane. "If I get in trouble at school again, my dad's gonna—"

He was interrupted by a sharp cry that ended as abruptly as it had begun.

They exchanged wide-eyed glances. Corey slunk to the mouth of the cave and peered down. "Holy shit, he fell. Trinkley fell, and I think he's dead!"

Shane was already clambering out of the cave. "We gotta get out of here. We didn't see anything, right? We were never here."

"Wait," said Laura. "What about the note? He might have it on him. If the police talk to Ms. Glotfelty, she won't know anything about it. And if they call in a handwriting expert, they'll figure out I'm the one who wrote it."

Shane chewed his lip like he was trying to figure out how this might not be his problem. In the end, he muttered, "Shit!" and led the way back to the main trail.

No one spoke as they walked. Shane stopped at a point where the trail disappeared around a bend. Bugbane Rock was just up ahead. Shane turned toward Laura without looking at her and said, "We'll wait here while you go see if he has the note on him."

Laura's mouth fell open. "What? You expect *me* to do it?"

"You're the one who wrote the note."

Laura glared at him. "Oh, that's nice, Shane. That's real nice. You're such a gentleman."

She sat down on a fallen log, making it clear she wasn't going anywhere.

"Guys, come on. We need to hurry," said Corey. "Somebody could show up at any minute."

And yet Corey didn't volunteer to check Trinkley's body for the note.

They were at a stalemate. Laura stared at Shane, Shane stared at the ground, and Corey threw anxious glances at all of them.

Duncan pushed past his friends. "Fine! I'll look for the note. But you're all coming with me."

Laura shook her head. "Not me. I don't want to see a dead body."

"Too bad, Laura—you're gonna see it. All of you are. It's our fault he died. The least we can do is look at him, maybe have a moment of silence. God." Duncan had never despised his little group more—and that included himself.

He rounded the curve, the others traipsing behind him. His throat constricted when he saw Trinkley lying on the rocks. The man's leg was bent at an impossible angle, and blood pooled under his head. Behind Duncan, somebody sobbed.

Something was poking out of Trinkley's shirt pocket, a slip of paper. Was it Laura's note? Duncan's heart thudded as he inched closer. He reached down and pinched the edge of the paper between his thumb and forefinger, being careful not to touch Trinkley's body. When the paper was out, he took a look. Yes, it was the note Laura had written.

A subtle movement drew his attention back to Trinkley. He gasped as he saw that the man's eyes were now open. *He wasn't dead!* Slowly, Trinkley's head turned toward him. Duncan backpedaled, trying to get away, but fell, landing hard on the unforgiving rock. Trinkley gave him a long look before shifting his gaze to the others. His mouth moved like he was trying to say something. Then he went still. His pupils dilated. Duncan knew he was gone, this time for real.

Without a word, the four of them sped away from the biggest horror they had ever known.

Chapter 28

Blake

"We need to track Ms. Glotfelty down," said Charlie. "She has to be at the next séance."

He was seated at the computer desk in his bedroom, scrolling through internet search results while Blake paced from wall to wall, door to window, wearing a hypothetical groove in the carpeting. Charlie had borrowed a chair from his sister's room so Blake could join him at the computer, but Blake was too restless to sit.

"The séance is tonight," Blake reminded his friend. "We're not going to find her before then."

"I realize that," said Charlie. "I'm saying we need to reschedule the séance."

Blake flashed Charlie a look of exasperation, which went unseen because Charlie's eyes were glued to his computer screen. "We can't reschedule—everything's set for tonight. Mr. Nolty and Mrs. Eppley agreed to come. If we reschedule, they might change their minds."

"They're not going to change their minds. Mrs. Eppley's daughter's life is on the line."

"C, come on! We can't afford to wait. Ava might be dying at this very moment."

Charlie threw Blake a dry look. "If Ava is dying at

this very moment, it's already too late to save her. But if we find Ms. Glotfelty, if she talks Trinkley into ending the curse, other people will be saved. Will, Zoe, Lonnie's mom. Everyone else who got a sucky destiny."

"But it could take days to track her down. Weeks. We might never find her."

"We have to try. Trinkley was obviously in love with Ms. Glotfelty. If anybody can talk him into ending the curse, it's her."

Blake stopped pacing long enough to peer over Charlie's shoulder at the computer screen. "Are you having any luck at all?"

"Not yet. But that doesn't mean we won't find her. If she got married, her name might be different. So here's what we'll do. I'll keep searching online. If I don't find anything by Monday, we'll talk to people at school. Mr. Perry, Principal Kouriki, maybe even Hank. We'll ask the current math teachers, too. Somebody's bound to know something." He nodded toward an old yearbook on the desk. "Let's take another look at that picture."

They'd borrowed the yearbook from Mr. Nolty so they could study Ms. Glotfelty's photo. Blake flipped to the Math Faculty pages, which Charlie had marked with an empty candy bar wrapper. The middle photo on the left page showed a thin, attractive young woman with long blonde hair and sculpted cheekbones standing in front of a blackboard covered in algebraic equations. The caption below the photo read, "Ms. Emily Glotfelty makes math as easy as pi!"

"She looks sad," Blake commented. Ms. Glotfelty was smiling, but it was a contrived smile, pasted on for the benefit of the camera.

"She probably was. This photo would have been taken after Trinkley died, and if she liked him as much as he liked her…" Charlie left the rest unsaid.

"Too bad she doesn't still teach at Pinedale Central High," Blake lamented.

That would have been the best-case scenario, but none of the school's current math teachers looked anything like Ms. Glotfelty, even when you factored in twenty years of aging.

"I'm going to try some different search terms," Charlie said, his fingers clacking away on the keyboard.

Blake trudged across the room and pondered a video game poster mounted on Charlie's closet door. The illustration depicted an attack from above—green laser beams shooting from purplish-black clouds, fiery explosions fracturing city buildings. Blake had never been able to beat Charlie at this particular game. Actually, he rarely beat Charlie at any game. It was annoying. In general, things tended to go Charlie's way most of the time.

He marched back to Charlie's desk. "If you want to keep searching for Ms. Glotfelty, that's great. I'm all for it. But I'm not canceling tonight's séance."

Charlie swiveled around in his chair. "But—"

"Uh!" Blake held up a hand, silencing him. "An apology from Mr. Nolty and Mrs. Eppley might be enough to get Trinkley to end the curse. And if it isn't—then we'll have another séance once we find Ms. Glotfelty."

Charlie got to his feet and loomed over Blake like a vampire. "Have you forgotten how hard it was to get an audience with Trinkley in the first place? If we keep having séances, he'll get sick of us bugging him. He won't even bother to show up."

"You don't know that."

"And you don't know that he'll appear like an obedient genie every time we summon him."

It occurred to Blake that he and Charlie would never see eye to eye on this issue. Well, no sense in prolonging the debate. He sidestepped his friend and headed for the door. "I need to get home for dinner. Mom's making chicken pot pie." He paused to look back at Charlie. "I'm having the séance with or without you. I'd rather do it with you. So are you in or are you out?"

Charlie's scowl consumed his entire face—forehead, eyebrows, eyes, mouth. Even his nose seemed to be frowning. He growled, "Fine. I'm in."

Blake jittered inwardly throughout dinner, dreading the séance. Summoning a belligerent ghost would never stop being scary. And he was pretty sure that with Ava out of the picture, he would end up having to lead the séance, something he'd never done before.

At a quarter till eight, he told his mom he was going over to Charlie's. It wasn't a lie. It was an incomplete truth.

When Charlie opened the front door, Blake knew at once that something was wrong. Charlie had a weird grimace on his face, and his eyes kept darting away.

"Aw, dude," Blake said reprovingly, as he jumped to the obvious conclusion. "Do not tell me you're bailing on me."

Charlie hung his head, uncharacteristically contrite. "I'm sorry, Blake. Really sorry. Something came up."

"Oh my God. Seriously?" He glared at Charlie.

"Let me guess. You got a new video game in the mail."

Charlie gave him a long, reproachful look. "That's not fair, man."

"Not fair? I'll tell you what's not fair—you bailing on me." Blake's fury was making him hot all over. He unzipped his jacket to let the cool nighttime air in. "I'm dying to hear the deets, bro. Dying to find out what's more important than saving your friends' lives."

Charlie pulled his gaze away. "It's complicated. We don't have time to discuss it right now."

"You were supposed to drive. Ava's spirit board is still in the trunk of your car."

"I can still drive you to the school. Come on, let's go."

Neither of them spoke during the short car ride. There seemed to be more tension than oxygen in the air, making it hard for Blake to breathe. As he collected the spirit board and the bag of candles from the trunk, Charlie stepped around the side of the car. "I still might be able to make it. If you can just hold off for a little while—"

"I'm not holding off." Blake slammed the trunk shut. "We told Mr. Nolty and Mrs. Eppley the séance would start at eight, and that's when we're having it. You go take care of your important business. Don't worry about us." He stormed off toward the school.

He found Mr. Nolty and Mrs. Eppley at the rear of the building, near the door leading into the science wing. They both looked terrible—sad and exhausted, with dark circles underscoring their eyes.

"Where's Charlie?" asked Mr. Nolty.

"He couldn't make it," said Blake. "It's fine. We don't need him." But he wondered if a séance would be as effective with only three people.

He held the door open for his companions. Mr. Nolty stepped through, but Mrs. Eppley hesitated. "So we're actually going to summon the ghost of a guy who hates us? A guy we killed?"

"We didn't kill him," Mr. Nolty reminded her. "His death was an accident. He shouldn't have tried to climb that cliff."

"That doesn't matter. He obviously blames us."

"I know it's scary," said Blake. "But we have to do this. To save Maddy." Personally, he didn't think Maddy could be saved, but Mrs. Eppley didn't need to know that.

Mrs. Eppley gave a resigned sigh and stepped into the building.

When they got upstairs to Mrs. Carr's room, Blake set up the spirit board on a student desk while Mrs. Eppley lit the candles. Then the three of them sat around the desk. Mr. Nolty and Mrs. Eppley had never attended a séance before, so Blake explained what it would entail. He showed them how to position their fingertips on the planchette.

"You ready?" he asked, and they both nodded. They looked like kids strapped into a death-defying roller coaster, waiting for the ride to begin.

"We are here tonight to contact the spirit of Mr. Larry Trinkley," Blake said, trying to mimic Ava's singsongy séance voice. He felt silly, though. Overdramatic, like a bad actor in a cheesy TV show. Then again, their situation was as dire as any TV melodrama, so he might as well give it his all. "Mr. Trinkley," he intoned, "if you're with us tonight, give us a sign. Speak to us from the spirit world."

Time ticked by—seconds, then minutes. The candles on Mrs. Carr's desk flickered gently, stirred by the forced-air heating. Outside, the darkness deepened as the moon slipped behind a woolly cloud. Blake felt nervous tension flowing around the desk like electricity.

He tried again. "Mr. Larry Trinkley, please show yourself. We come to you tonight with a matter of great urgency."

He glanced around the room. Shadows filled every corner, thick as mud. But nothing emerged from those pockets of darkness, and only the most ordinary of noises broke the silence: the hum of the heater, the creak of seats as people fidgeted, the whistling of Mr. Nolty's nostril each time he inhaled.

"This is pointless," said Mrs. Eppley. "He's not going to come."

"Last time it took a while," said Blake. "We need to be patient." He decided to try a different tactic. "Robert, are you there? Robert, please show yourself. You found Mr. Trinkley for us once. Can you do it again?"

"Who the hell is Robert?" asked Mr. Nolty. Mrs. Eppley shushed him.

"Robert, we need you. Please join us."

At the previous séance, Ava had addressed her plea to spirits at large, and Robert happened to be the one who'd shown up. Maybe he wasn't the only one who could help them, thought Blake.

"Spirits of Pinedale Central High, I ask you to join our circle. We welcome anyone who can hear this plea."

Nobody showed up. Beyond the window, a silvery glow suffused the sky as the moon emerged from the cloud.

Blake was beginning to harbor serious doubts about his ability to summon spirits. Maybe it was a talent not everyone had. Ava, clearly, was a natural. He, Blake, was not.

He gave Mr. Nolty and Mrs. Eppley a tight, apologetic smile. "The ghosts don't seem to be biting tonight. Would one of you like to try?"

"Like that would make a difference." Mr. Nolty got to his feet, staggering a little. It occurred to Blake that he was drunk—but that was no surprise. These days, Mr. Nolty always seemed to be drunk.

"We should at least try," said Blake.

"Kid, we already tried. We failed. I don't have time for this crap. I'm going home."

Blake said, "Home to your whiskey bottle?" Instantly he winced, regretting the jab.

Mr. Nolty gave him a murderous look. "You little snot." He stomped toward the door.

"I'm sorry!" Blake said. "I shouldn't have said that. I'm just—frustrated."

Mr. Nolty held up a hand like he didn't want to hear it.

Mrs. Eppley called, "Duncan, please don't go! This might be our only chance to save Maddy."

Mr. Nolty halted in the doorway, his thin frame stooped like a gnarled old apple tree. He glanced back at Blake and scowled again. But his eyes softened as they fell on Mrs. Eppley. He gave a begrudging nod and stepped back into the room. Blake released a long, tense breath.

Mr. Nolty sauntered down the first aisle of the classroom, thumping a hand on each desk as he passed.

"Do you know this is the first time I've been in this building since the night I graduated? The whole time Deej was in school, I never once showed up for parents' night. Never attended a Christmas concert or a parent-teacher conference. I couldn't bring myself to walk through those doors. To face those memories of what we did to Mr. Trinkley." He threw a glance at Maddy's mom. "How about you, Laura? You been back?"

Mrs. Eppley spoke softly. "Yeah, I've been back. I come for the concerts, for parents' night, for parent-teacher conferences. I come for it all because Maddy wants me to. She'd be disappointed if I refused. She wouldn't understand."

Mr. Nolty gave a short laugh. "You're a better parent than I ever was."

No one argued with that.

"It isn't easy," Mrs. Eppley added. "Every time I set foot in this building, it sends me into a funk that lasts for days."

Mr. Nolty turned a corner and strolled up an aisle toward the front of the classroom. "In my day there were blackboards. Now there are whiteboards. I wonder what else has changed."

"A lot," said Mrs. Eppley. "A lot has changed in twenty years." And she proceeded to tell him about some of the things she'd noticed.

As she spoke, an uneasy feeling crept over Blake, a sense of being watched by invisible eyes. Maybe it was his imagination, but the room seemed cooler than it had been when they'd arrived. Were ghosts lurking in the shadows, curious and elusive like fish trying not to get caught?

"We should try again," he said when the talk

between Mrs. Eppley and Mr. Nolty petered out. Mr. Nolty returned to his chair. Neither adult volunteered to lead the séance, so Blake supposed it was up to him again.

"Larry Trinkley," he said, "we invite you to join our circle. Duncan and Laura are with us tonight, and they wish to speak to you about that day at Bugbane Rock. The day you died."

His breath hitched as a massive chill overtook the room. The candle flames leapt, casting warped shadows on the walls.

"God help us," whispered Mrs. Eppley, making the sign of the cross.

Blake gripped the edges of the desk as he steeled himself for whatever was to come. Even so, he couldn't suppress a gasp as Mr. Trinkley materialized in a corner by the whiteboard, transparent and glowing. Maddy's mom and Deej's dad huddled together, exhaling frosted puffs of air as they beheld the man they'd driven to his death.

Mr. Trinkley did not look pleased to have been summoned. His fists were clenched. His ghostly glow pulsed furiously. Malevolence oozed from his eyes.

Blake stood up, his knees knocking so hard that he expected them to give out at any moment. "Mr. Trinkley, thank you for coming. As you can see, Duncan and Laura are here. They have some things they wish to say to you." He dropped back into his chair, relieved to be turning the program over to the two adults.

An arctic wind with no logical source swept the classroom. It flowed over Blake's face, chilling his cheeks. A small stack of papers on Mrs. Carr's desk rustled.

Mr. Nolty stood up, shaking visibly. "Mr. Trinkley, I—I—I want to, you know, apologize." His Adam's apple bobbed as he swallowed hard. "I'm so sorry about what happened to you at Bugbane Rock. God knows, not a day has gone by since then that I haven't—"

He broke off as the wind blew the candles out. The gale force was intensifying. The papers on Mrs. Carr's desk flew into the air and flapped around like disembodied wings. Mr. Trinkley stared balefully from the corner.

"You didn't deserve to die," Mr. Nolty continued. "We never should have—"

A vase of flowers on Mrs. Carr's desk toppled to the floor and shattered. Mrs. Eppley's hair swirled around her head like a nest of tethered snakes.

"You have to understand," Mr. Nolty shouted, trying to be heard over the roar of the wind, "we were just a bunch of hot-headed, immature kids who—"

Three chairs blew over. A round clock fell off the wall. A window shade sailed across the room and slammed into the wall.

"We never meant—"

Books flew off shelves and fluttered through the air like obese butterflies. A fluorescent light crashed to the floor.

Mr. Nolty yelped and dove under a desk. Blake and Mrs. Eppley followed suit. The room was a tornado of flying objects—books, papers, candles, chairs. A metal waste can. Several calculators. Two pairs of scissors. It was worse than a rogue hailstorm.

"Stop! Please stop!" screamed Mrs. Eppley, covering her ears with both hands. "We're sorry, Mr.

Trinkley! Truly sorry! Won't you please end the curse?"

Mr. Trinkley swelled to impossible proportions, his face contorted in rage. "Sins of the fathers!" he thundered, and then he vanished with an explosive boom.

The wind ceased abruptly. Blake stayed put for a few minutes, making sure the tempest was over. Then he crawled out from under the desk, his knees crunching over broken glass. He heard Mrs. Eppley weeping softly. The wreckage of Mrs. Carr's room was visible in the moonlight. He couldn't imagine what the school authorities would make of it.

From the doorway someone said, "Holy crap."

It was Charlie. And he wasn't alone.

Chapter 29

Charlie

"What happened here?" Charlie asked, his voice an incredulous squeak. He flicked the lights on so he could see better. The room looked like the aftermath of a hurricane.

In a few terse sentences, Blake told him about the evening's events. Charlie refrained from saying *I told you so* but allowed himself the luxury of thinking it. He'd known it would take more than an apology to get Trinkley to back down.

Mrs. Martinetti, the computer science teacher, stood at Charlie's side shaking her head dazedly. "So much destruction! And all this was done by a ghost?"

Blake pulled Charlie over to the whiteboard for a whispered conversation. "What's she doing here? I thought we agreed not to drag innocent people into this."

"She's not innocent people. She's Ms. Glotfelty."

Blake gasped so theatrically that the adults in the room turned to look at him. "Mrs. Martinetti is Ms. Glotfelty? But that's impossible! She doesn't look anything like Ms. Glotfelty. Her face is rounder. Her hair is different."

"People gain weight. Hairstyles change."

"Ms. Glotfelty taught math. Mrs. Martinetti is a

computer teacher."

"Blake, I know it's hard to wrap your head around this, but trust me—it's true."

Blake stared hard at Mrs. Martinetti, as if trying to see the young woman from that long-ago yearbook photo. He gave up with a shake of his head. "How'd you figure it out?"

"I kept looking at that picture of Ms. Glotfelty in the yearbook. Something about her eyes seemed familiar. It finally hit me that Mrs. Martinetti has those same eyes. Sad and thoughtful and kind all at the same time. So I looked up her address. I went to her house. I asked if she used to be Ms. Glotfelty, and she said yes. I told her about Trinkley and the curse, and she agreed to help us."

Blake kicked at a shard of broken vase on the floor. "Why'd you keep it from me, C? Why didn't you tell me where you were going tonight?"

"I didn't want to get your hopes up. Hell, I didn't want to get *my* hopes up. I seriously didn't expect it to pan out."

Blake sent another glance Mrs. Martinetti's way. "Are you sure it's her? Her name is different. Not just her last name. Her first name, too."

"Dude, I'll tell you everything later, I promise. Come on, we need to get the séance started."

Charlie walked over to the séance desk, where the three adults were conversing quietly. "You can sit here," he told Mrs. Martinetti. She slid into the chair Blake had been using. Her nose was very red.

There'd been a lot of crying on the way to the school, and not just by Mrs. Martinetti. Tears had sprung to Charlie's eyes a couple of times as he'd listened to her story. She'd been in love with Mr. Trinkley, but he'd died before their romance could get off the ground. Compounding her grief was the sense that she'd lost her soulmate, the one and only man she would ever love.

Her life in those first few months had been unbearable, the sadness so deep that it seemed to be entwined around her organs. She longed to be someone different, a person untouched by tragedy. She wanted to make a fresh start. She thought about leaving town, but her entire extended family lived in Pinedale, and she needed their love and support more than ever.

So she decided to make some smaller changes, beginning with her name. She'd always gone by her first name, Emily. Now she used her middle name, Rose. It took a while for people to get used to it, but eventually the new name stuck. When she got married five years later, her last name changed as well.

Going to work each day was torture, especially at first. Memories haunted the math wing, playing behind her eyes like clips from a sappy old movie. Those daily talks, the playful flirting. She asked the school administrators if a transfer to a different department was possible. She'd always been good with computers, and she took a few college courses to further develop her skills. The following year she was Pinedale Central High School's newest computer science teacher.

She stopped dying her hair blonde and let its natural color, chestnut brown, grow in. She got her hair cut.

Even with all the changes it had been a long, difficult road—but she'd made it. She'd found love again, which had led to marriage and motherhood. She had a job she adored, a lively group of friends. Rose Martinetti had made a rich, full life for herself.

But now, suddenly, a scab had been torn off a wound that had never really healed. And that was why she couldn't stop crying.

Charlie understood. He just hoped she wouldn't be too distraught to speak to Mr. Trinkley.

"We should get those candles relit," said Mrs. Eppley.

She and Charlie walked around the room picking up the fallen candles, several of which had broken during the Trinkley tornado. They salvaged what they could, and Charlie relit them. He turned off the lights and sat at Mrs. Carr's desk. Mrs. Eppley returned to her seat, and Blake pulled a fourth chair up to the séance desk.

"Mr. Trinkley was pretty mad when he left," said Mr. Nolty. "He might not come back."

Charlie shrugged. "All we can do is try."

Over the next fifteen minutes, Blake made increasingly desperate pleas to the school's spirit population, including Mr. Trinkley, Robert, and anyone else who might be listening. In between, there were long periods of silence. Nothing happened, other than the heater clicking on and off and the moon gliding in and out of clouds. Charlie thought about offering to take over for Blake, but he didn't think he would be any better at summoning spirits.

Finally Mrs. Martinetti spoke up. "Let me try." She tilted her face up and stared into the darkness above the whiteboard. Her voice rang out, rich and clear: "Larry Trinkley, are you there? It's me—Emily."

That was when everything stilled, like machinery

whirring to a halt. The heater stopped humming. The candle flames stopped flickering. It was as if the room itself was listening, an entity in its own right. Charlie nodded at Mrs. Martinetti, urging her to keep going.

"Larry? Is that you? Oh, my dear, how I've missed you! I've thought of you so often over the years. I wish things had been different. I know that if you had lived, you and I would have had something very special."

And then she launched into a narrative monologue, as if dictating a letter to a long-lost friend. She said she was married now and had two sons, ages eleven and thirteen. The younger one thought he might want to be a teacher someday, while the older one was so articulate and charismatic that she was sure he'd end up being a politician or a talk show host.

She bewailed the advent of new math. She was no longer a math teacher but had kept abreast of the changes over the years. Some were okay, but others seemed unnecessary. She was sure Larry would agree. The old teaching methods had worked just fine. Why fix something that wasn't broken?

Tears glistened in her eyes as she looked back on her friendship with Mr. Trinkley. Their conversations had been the highlight of her workdays. She'd especially appreciated his dry sense of humor, which was so much like her own.

She remembered the day he'd died, how they'd talked at lunchtime about an actor they both admired. They'd named his movies one by one and argued good-naturedly about which was the best. When Larry mentioned that the actor's new movie would be coming out soon, she'd made a secret, fervent wish that he would invite her to see it with him. What a wonderful first date that would have been.

As Charlie listened to Mrs. Martinetti talk, his heart grew heavy. Before tonight it had never occurred to him that there'd been people in Mr. Trinkley's life who'd loved him. People who missed him and still mourned his death. Maybe Mr. Trinkley hadn't been a monster after all, just an ordinary man with good and bad in him. He probably hadn't gone into teaching with the aim of alienating his students. It had just happened. He'd gotten off on the wrong foot and had never been able to recover.

Charlie was so deep in thought that he didn't notice the temperature dropping until his teeth started chattering. He looked around, momentarily disoriented, and gave a start when he saw Mr. Trinkley hovering in the corner by the whiteboard, his ghostly glow outshining the candles.

Mrs. Martinetti let out a slow, reverent breath. "Larry. There you are."

An anguished moan resounded through the room. Mr. Trinkley's eyes latched onto Mrs. Martinetti, his expression stricken. His mouth moved—*no, no, no*. Charlie got the sense that he was drinking her in and pushing her away at the same time.

"I know," whispered Mrs. Martinetti, wiping tears from her eyes. "I know this is hard for you. It's hard for me, too."

She left her seat and walked toward Mr. Trinkley, her arms outstretched. As she got close, Mr. Trinkley zoomed away like a skittish bird.

Mrs. Martinetti followed him across the room, stepping over fallen books and pushing toppled chairs aside. "Larry, listen to me. I want you to end the curse."

Mr. Trinkley's mouth twisted in dismay as he looked back to see Mrs. Martinetti trailing him. He fled to the rear of the room. Charlie prayed he wouldn't disappear.

"None of those twenty-three kids ever did anything to you," Mrs. Martinetti went on, veering down the nearest aisle in steady pursuit. "And the kids who did have been punished enough. Two of them are dead. The other two have suffered mightily."

A sob from Mrs. Eppley punctuated that statement.

"I understand your anger," Mrs. Martinetti said. "I truly do. But you've let it fester to the point where it's become something huge and malignant. Something out of proportion to the original wrong that was done to you."

Mr. Trinkley pressed himself into a corner. His glow was dimming, and it pulsed slower and slower, like a waning heartbeat.

"Those kids never intended for you to die," said Mrs. Martinetti, reaching the rear of the classroom. "Your death was an accident. A tragic accident. Don't you realize that?"

This time Mr. Trinkley didn't flee. He watched with resigned eyes as Mrs. Martinetti walked up to him.

"I remember a man with a big heart," said Mrs. Martinetti, managing a tremulous smile despite the tears that streamed down her cheeks. "A sweet, kind man who brought me coffee and doughnuts every Friday morning. A man who once saved a baby bird that had fallen out of a tree behind the school. That's the man I fell in love with. I have to believe he still exists."

Mr. Trinkley opened his mouth like he wanted to say something, but he couldn't seem to get the words out. He shook his head in frustration. Charlie wondered if the earlier tantrum had sapped his ghostly energy.

"It's time to let go of your anger. Time to end the curse and move on. Can you do that, Larry? Can you do it for me?"

Mr. Trinkley's mouth trembled as he ran a hand down Mrs. Martinetti's cheek. He nodded heavily and turned to face the others. His eyes brimmed with shame and remorse, as if he finally saw the unjustness of the suffering he'd caused. He mouthed, *Forgive me.* The air around him crackled as he faded away to nothing.

For a full minute, no one spoke. Mrs. Martinetti collapsed against the wall, sobs racking her body. Mr. Nolty asked in a shaky voice, "Is that it? Is the curse over?"

Blake patted his jacket pocket. He reached inside and pulled out a rectangular object. "My cell phone's back!"

Mrs. Eppley jumped up. "Oh! Maybe Maddy's back, too!"

"I wouldn't count on it," said a voice from the rear of the room.

Charlie watched as a glowing form detached itself from the shadows. Robert wafted toward them.

The three adults stared in fascination. Charlie introduced them to Robert.

"The simpler curses can be reversed pretty quickly," Robert said. "But some of the others might take a while. And some might have progressed to the point where they can't be undone at all."

"Oh my God. Maddy!" cried Mrs. Eppley. "I have to go. I have to see if—"

She rushed out of the room. Mrs. Martinetti

followed, calling, "Laura, wait."

Charlie watched them go, his newfound joy evaporating. If Maddy and Ava didn't make it out of this alive— But he couldn't bear to think about that.

"How long will it take for all the individual curses to end?" Blake asked Robert.

"Hard to say. I'd give it a few weeks."

"Where'd Mr. Trinkley go?" asked Mr. Nolty. "Is he still haunting the school?"

Robert twirled slowly in a circle, his arms stretched in front of him like divining rods. "I don't sense him anymore. He might be gone for good." He glanced at the wall clock, still ticking away though it now lay on the floor, its plastic frame cracked. "Speaking of *gone*, I gotta skedaddle, too. Got a janitor to haunt."

His voice dropped to a growl. "I can't stand that guy. He's nothing like Hank. He's always cutting corners, mopping around things instead of pushing them out of the way. Sneaks naps in the teacher's lounge, too. His work ethic sucks." He caught Charlie's eye and winked. "*Sucks.* I know you guys still use that one." Instead of disappearing, he sailed through the wall into the hallway.

"Well. I guess that's that," said Charlie. But he frowned uneasily as he glanced around. The room was abnormally cold, even though Robert and Mr. Trinkley were gone.

Chapter 30

Blake

Blake packed the spirit board and planchette into their box while Charlie gathered up the candles. Mr. Nolty waited by the door. Charlie had offered to give him a ride home since Mrs. Eppley had left without him.

"Let's get out of here, C," Blake said, heading for the door. He glanced behind him, but Charlie wasn't coming. He was rooted in place, staring into the shadows at the rear of the classroom.

"Charlie? Come on, bro, let's go."

Charlie shook his head, his mouth hanging open.

Blake followed his gaze. And he saw…he saw…

"Deej?" His voice cracked in astonishment. "Oh my God, is that you?"

Deej drifted up to them, flashing his usual devilish grin. "Just stopping by to prove that *dead* doesn't always mean *gone*."

"Oh my God. *Oh my God!*" Blake rushed forward to hug his friend but stepped right through him instead.

"Dude, I'm not solid anymore," said Deej. "Try to adapt."

Blake heard a choked cry behind him. "Deej? Oh, my boy. My precious boy! I'm so sorry this happened to you. So sorry you died." Mr. Nolty sobbed as if his heart was breaking, which it surely was.

"It's okay, Dad," said Deej. "I'm okay. Think of it this way: I'm proof of an afterlife. That's good news, right?"

But Mr. Nolty could not be consoled. Deej wafted around the room while his dad cried it out. Meanwhile, Blake and Charlie peppered him with questions.

"Did it hurt when you died?"

"Nah, it was real quick."

"What's it like being dead?"

"It's fine. Just—different."

"So you're haunting the school now?"

"Yeah. At least till you guys graduate. That way I can still see you. I can follow you through the halls. I can hear what you talk about."

"But aren't you lonely? It sounds lonely."

"Lonely?" A snort. "No, I'm not lonely. Let's just say there's more to this building than meets the eye."

And then it was Deej's turn to ask *them* a question. "So…Maddy. Has she turned up?"

Blake and Charlie exchanged uncomfortable glances. Charlie said, "Not yet, man."

The crestfallen look on Deej's face seemed to go beyond concern for a friend. Blake wondered if Deej had a thing for Maddy. He'd wondered for a while, actually.

"We're not giving up hope," he added. "Now that the curse has ended, she might turn up soon."

But there was no real hope in his voice or in his heart. Maddy had been gone for three weeks. Her kidnapper would have had plenty of opportunities to murder her.

Finally, Mr. Nolty ran out of steam. He wiped his

eyes on his jacket sleeve and turned to Deej. "I miss you, son. I miss you so much."

Deej floated close to his father. "I miss you, too, Dad. But we're together now, so let's make the most of it. We have lots to talk about. You and me, we've never talked that much."

Mr. Nolty nodded heavily. "That's on me. I wish— I wish I could go back and do it all over. God, I was such a jerk! I was so preoccupied with my own problems that I never had time for you."

"It's okay. Now I understand why you always seemed so tormented. So determined to self-destruct. But the Mr. Trinkley thing is finally over. It's over, Dad, and it's time you got your shit together. You need to stop drinking. You need to stop hooking up with skanks. You need—" Deej got in his dad's face, like an army sergeant berating a private. "You need to focus on making a good life for yourself."

Mr. Nolty wept softly into his hands. "I don't deserve a good life."

"Sure you do. You absolutely do."

It occurred to Blake that he and Charlie shouldn't be listening in on such a personal conversation. "Hey, Deej?" he said. "Charlie and I are going to take off. That is, if it's okay with your dad." He turned to Mr. Nolty. "Do you have another way to get home?"

Mr. Nolty nodded. "I'll get my dad to drive me. Better yet, maybe I'll walk. I could use the exercise, a chance to clear my head."

"Hey guys?" said Deej as Blake and Charlie turned to go. "Anytime you want to hang out, stop by my locker—preferably after school or in the evening when nobody's around. If I'm not there, give a holler. I'll hear."

Blake nodded. "We'll do that, D. We'll do it soon."

"You'd better. 'Cause if you don't, I'll haunt your sorry asses."

Chapter 31

Lonnie's mom

Inertia pressed Julia Turko to the left as she rounded the highway exit ramp. Her headlights swung across a small, bald tree, some twiggy shrubbery, and the glowing eyes of a night creature, a possum or a raccoon. She came to a stop—sort of—at the bottom of the ramp, threw a perfunctory glance over her left shoulder, and pulled onto the two-lane road that would take her back to Pinedale. Twenty more minutes and she would be home, ready to stream the latest episode of her favorite TV show. First, though, she needed to stop at her sister's house to drop off a kitten. This was a surprise for her daughter Lonnie's birthday, and it wasn't the kind of gift you could hide in your bedroom closet for four days.

Meow! Meow! Meow!

The kitten hadn't shut up since Julia had left the breeder's place in Raleigh. She hoped this wasn't an indication of what life with a cat was going to be like. Was incessant meowing a Persian cat thing? If so, she would just have to suck it up, because *Persian cat* was the only acceptable pet choice. Lonnie had been obsessed with Persians since the age of ten. She had pictures of them taped to her bedroom walls and a whole shelf of books about them. She collected Persian cat figurines. Her favorite sweatshirt had a picture of a Persian cat on the front.

Meow, meow, meow!

"Shut up!" Julia hollered at the pet carrier in the back seat. "Sheesh! We'll be there soon."

This kitten would be the biggest surprise of Lonnie's life. Julia's four children had begged for a pet repeatedly over the years, but Julia and her husband, Greg, had resisted. They weren't pet people, and the house was chaotic enough with six humans in it. Of course, there were exceptions. A goldfish won by a nine-year-old at the county fair was okay because those little critters never lasted long. An occasional weekend visit from the middle-school science-room gerbil? Also fine. But that was where they'd drawn the line.

Until now.

The kitten was Julia's last hope. If that pee-scented, caterwauling ball of fur didn't snap Lonnie out of her funk—well, the next step would involve mental health professionals. Therapy, antidepressants, shock treatments, whatever it took.

The whole thing was humiliating. Both Julia and Greg came from sturdy mental stock. No one in their respective families had ever suffered from mental illness. How had this happened? Had they taken the wrong baby home from the hospital?

Lonnie was their firstborn, and she'd been the mellowest baby, the sweetest toddler, the sunniest six-year-old. She'd sailed through puberty with barely a scowl. Then, a month or so ago, she'd changed abruptly. Now she was a tortured soul who moped around the house not talking to anyone and bursting into tears at odd moments.

She was clingy, too. She constantly begged Julia not to leave the house, even when Julia had important places to be, like work or yoga class or an appointment at the hair salon. Sometimes she would throw herself into Julia's arms, sobbing, "I'm sorry!" without explaining what she was sorry about.

"You've got your work cut out for you, Meowy McMeowsterson," Julia told the kitten. "Don't let me down."

One of those non-melodious modern songs came on the radio. Ugh. Julia switched to another station, and then another, before finding a song from ten years ago that she sort of liked. As a rule, she tried to stay in touch with today's music so she could bond with her kids over it. But so much of it was crap, vastly inferior to the tunes Julia had grown up with.

She sang along with the old song, drowning out the kitten's meows. But just as the refrain began, the radio went haywire, changing from station to station of its own accord. In the back seat, the kitten hissed.

Something buzzed against Julia's ear, sending an unpleasant tingle down her spine. It sounded like a largish insect, but how could that be? It was late November, and most of the insects were either dead or hunkered down for the winter in underground hidey-holes.

She switched on the car's interior light and saw a bee heading straight for her face. She shrieked and ducked her head. The bee circled around and attacked from a new direction. And, oh God, now it was on top of her head, and if it got tangled in her hair, it would sting her scalp, so she shook her head like crazy and reached up with both hands trying to flick it away, and when she glanced up, she saw that her car had drifted into the oncoming lane. A big truck hurtled toward her, just a few feet away, and her hands were too far from the steering wheel—

—and then somehow she was back in her own lane, and the truck sped past, blaring its horn to decry her reckless driving, and everything was fine.

Except not really. She was so shaken that she pulled off the road. She was in a rural area, dried-up corn fields on both sides of the road, though she couldn't see much of them in the dark. No other cars were around. She ran her fingers hastily through her hair, but nothing fell out. She unbuckled her seatbelt and looked around. The bee was nowhere to be seen—or heard. But where had it gone? All the windows were up.

The radio had somehow switched itself off, and even the kitten had quieted down. The only sound was Julia's ragged breathing.

She replayed that minute over and over in her mind, trying to make sense of it. The buzzing bee, the looming truck, the unattended steering wheel. She should be dead, and yet she wasn't. But how had she gotten back into her own lane?

It was a mystery she would never solve.

Chapter 32

Maddy

Tommy no longer called her Rachel. Now he called her Madeline. When Maddy's mom called her Madeline, it usually meant she was in trouble. She was pretty sure the same applied here.

She really needed to find that hypothetical tool.

She knew the odds weren't good. Whatever those other girls had used to carve their names into the wood was probably long gone. But Maddy Eppley wasn't about to sit around like a death row prisoner waiting to be snuffed. As long as her heart was beating, she would never give up trying to save herself.

Funny, she'd never been like this before. She'd always been bland and passive, a victim of her own life rather than its master. But not anymore. If she was going to get out of this alive, she would have to make some big moves.

All week long, Tommy had worked the day shift. Today, Maddy devoted her afternoon to combing the cellar more thoroughly than she'd ever done before. She checked the walls for hidden niches. She searched the nook under the stairs, ignoring the cobwebs that clung to her hair. She probed the crack beneath that mysterious locked door. She stood on her chair and groped along the narrow ledges below the two windows. She moved around the cellar like a robot vacuum cleaner, using her eyes to scour every inch of the floor.

And then she did it all again. And again.

The third time around she noticed something that had been there all along but had never really registered with her. A drain in the floor. The circular drain cover was so obscured by filth and rust that she couldn't discern its original color. It was dotted with round holes, like Swiss cheese but more uniform. Maddy inserted a finger into one of those slimy holes (ick!) and pulled. The drain cover popped out of the floor.

Peering into that opening, she gave a gasp of joy, because there, lying across the drainpipe, was a metal fingernail file, four inches long and a quarter of an inch wide. This was it—the hidden tool! She snatched it up and dropped the drain cover back into place. The nail file had some orange rust on it, and the pointy end was dull—probably from all the wood-carving those girls had done—but otherwise it was in good shape.

Maddy didn't even consider carving her name below the others. There had to be a better use for this tool. But what? She supposed she could try to stab Tommy, but how much damage could a flimsy nail file do? She would probably just make him mad, and then he would pump her full of bullets. Could she use the nail file to unlock the door at the top of the stairs? Doubtful. The tip was too big to fit into the lock on the doorknob. Ditto for the padlock on the wooden door in the cellar.

She paced the floor in frustration. There had to be something she could do. Some way to use this scrap of metal to save herself.

She came to a halt in front of the wooden door, contemplating it as she so often did. What was in there? Decomposing bodies? A torture chamber? Hopefully, something useful—a hammer, a crowbar, an ax. Some sort of weapon she could use against Tommy. She couldn't imagine herself swinging an ax at another human being, but if that was what it took to survive, by God she would do it.

She stepped closer to the door, examining it. The metal plate behind the padlock was screwed into the wood, and the screws were slotted roundheads. Maddy knew her screw types because Ron was a carpenter, and he liked to explain his craft to her when she hung out in his woodshop to watch him work.

She looked at the nail file in her hand. She saw how it might double as a screwdriver.

Tommy would be home from work soon and would bring her dinner shortly afterward. It would make sense to wait till he left for work tomorrow so she could take her time trying to remove the padlock. But could she afford to wait? No. Because what if today was the day he decided to murder her?

It was time to make that big move.

She inserted the blunt end of the nail file into the slot on the first screw and gave a hard twist. The screw was so rusted, it wouldn't budge. The second screw was also tight, but she managed to unscrew it. The third one came out easily. The fourth one was as stuck as the first.

She grunted with effort as she tried to turn those two stubborn screws, but they were as good as welded into place. In desperation, she slid the nail file under the metal plate and shimmied it around, trying to loosen the plate. She froze as she heard a car's motor rumble to a stop outside. Tommy was home.

She sawed the nail file wildly back and forth and finally felt the metal plate shift. Yes, it was definitely looser. She grabbed hold of the padlock and tugged, heartened to find there was some give to it now. With each yank, the metal plate screeched in protest as it slowly released its grip on the wood.

Maddy thought of her family, and that made her tug harder. Then she thought of Deej and gave an even harder yank. She really needed to see him. Since the beginning of the school year, he'd been looking at her in an unusual way. Not staring, because that would have been creepy. Just looking. And she'd been looking back.

The situation warranted further investigation.

She gritted her teeth and pulled as hard as she could with both hands. The wood of the old door splintered with a loud crack. The force of it sent her reeling, but she managed not to fall.

She looked down. Clutched in her hand like an extracted tooth was the padlock, still attached to the metal plate and a jagged hunk of wood. A gaping hole in the door marked the spot where the padlock plate had been. She saw that mildew had rotted the wood.

Had Tommy heard that splintering sound? Impossible to know, but she'd better not dawdle. Now that the door was conspicuously damaged, she had no choice but to follow through. She pulled the door open, cringing at its loud creak, and stepped into the room beyond it.

She groped along the wall, found a light switch, and flicked it on. She was in a small furnace room. An oil furnace and a water heater stood next to each other just inside the door. The rest of the room was empty. High on the far wall was a small wooden door, maybe fifteen inches square. Maddy knew immediately what it was: an opening for shoveling coal into the cellar. Her grandparents lived in a very old house, and they had a door like this in their furnace room, though they, like Tommy, no longer had a coal furnace.

Wow. This was better than any weapon.

She trotted back to the main part of the cellar to fetch the card table. When she shoved it against the wall in the furnace room, she saw that it wasn't high enough to put her in reach of the coal door. She went back for the chair. She had just picked it up when she heard the familiar creak of the ceiling. Tommy was coming.

She raced to the furnace room and placed the chair on top of the table. She scrambled onto the table and then onto the chair, praying that the flimsy card table would support her weight. The cellar door opened. Footsteps clomped down the stairs.

The coal door was latched from the inside with a simple hook lock. Maddy unlatched it and pulled the door open. It was going to take a lot of upper body strength to hoist herself up the wall and through that opening. She wasn't sure she could do it. If she couldn't—well then, she would swing the chair at Tommy when he entered the furnace room. She would kick him and bite him and pummel him with her fists, and if she got shot in the process, so be it. At least she would go down fighting.

Tommy swore, his voice alarmingly close by. Maddy heard a crash as he dropped the food tray.

She grasped the edges of the door frame with both hands and pulled herself up, up, up, her feet scrambling for traction on the concrete-block wall. Footsteps pattered into the furnace room.

"Stop right there!" bellowed Tommy, and Maddy cringed, certain she was about to be shot. But she kept going. She heaved her body all the way through the little doorway and rolled onto the ground outside.

Immediately, she jumped to her feet and took off running. It was twilight time, still light enough that she could see her surroundings. She was in a rural area, just as she'd thought. Tommy's shabby two-story house stood behind her, and in front of her a longish driveway led to a country lane. A thick woods obscured her view to the left. To the right of Tommy's yard was a rolling field, beyond which lay a stretch of woods. On the far side of the woods, on a hilltop, was a house, lights blazing through myriad windows. That was where she needed to go. But she couldn't take a shortcut through the field. The rightmost edge of Tommy's yard abutted a deep gully that would be difficult to cross. Taking the road would be quicker and easier.

She sprinted down the driveway and turned right onto the road. She knew Tommy might come after her in his car, so when she reached the stretch of woods, she tried to veer into it, seeking concealment among the trees. That turned out to be a no-go. A formidable tangle of brambles made the woods impossible to enter. She was forced to stay on the road.

Adrenaline was Maddy's friend, granting the gift of superhuman endurance. She felt as though she could run forever. She sped around a curve, raced down a straight stretch, and rounded another curve. And there was the house on the hill, tantalizingly close by, shining like a beacon in the gathering dusk.

She never heard the car coming until it sped out of the curve. She whirled around to face it, frozen like a small animal about to become roadkill. The car's headlights blinded her the same way Tommy's headlights had blinded her the night she'd been taken.

Chapter 33

Ava

"Hey, Ava, time to check your vitals."

Elijah was Ava's favorite nurse, not that it was much of a contest. She'd had only two nurses so far, and they were as different as night and day, just like their shifts. Elijah was on duty today and had also been here yesterday morning, when she'd been brought to the hospital. He was not only kind and friendly and funny and smart but also easy on the eyes, a real snack. His loose smile, that choco-licious gaze, the healthy sheen of his dark brown skin. As crushes went, this one would never amount to anything, because, number one, Elijah was a good ten years older than Ava, and number two, the gold band on his ring finger said he was spoken for. But she sure did enjoy looking at him.

Mona was the night nurse. Chronically crabby, perpetually pursed, with a crease like a half-drawn exclamation point between her eyebrows. Maybe she didn't like working nights. Maybe she hated teenagers. Ava hoped to be discharged before Mona's seven p.m. shift began.

"So, when do you think I can go home?" she asked her favorite nurse.

Elijah put his hands on his hips in mock indignation. "Can't wait to get away from me, huh?"

He winked and added, more seriously, "That's up to the doctor, sweetness. Enjoy it while you can. How often do you get to lie around in bed letting people take care of you?"

"Like never. You're right—I should chill," said Ava.

Elijah took her blood pressure, pulse, and temperature and pronounced everything fab-u-loso. He moved the TV remote from the nightstand to the bed, close to her hand. "Channel eight runs old movies every afternoon, if you're interested." He headed for the door, then paused to look back. "You need more pain meds?"

"No, I'm good." Her ankle throbbed, but she could stand it. The pain meds made her loopy, and she needed to have her wits about her when visitors came. There'd been a steady stream of them yesterday afternoon—especially after school let out—and a few more this morning. It was fun being the center of attention, getting showered with magazines and stuffed animals and other overpriced doodads from the hospital gift shop. She felt like a celebrity. She'd even been interviewed by a reporter from the local newspaper.

But was all the fuss worth the ordeal she'd gone through? Abso-freakin-lutely not.

When she thought back on that day, the day it had happened, the whole thing seemed hazy and surreal, like some weird TV show she'd watched long ago. The day had started out like any other Saturday. Her dad, mom, and brother had been out in the world doing their respective things, so after dance class she'd had the house to herself. Just past noon she'd answered a knock at the front door (after peeking out the window to make sure a kidnapper hadn't come to call). There on her porch stood her neighbor Mrs. Figard, holding a vase of flowers.

"Ava—hi, dear, I'm glad you're home. Here. Take them." She opened the screen door and thrust the vase at Ava. Ava started to ask why, but Mrs. Figard talked right over her.

"Birthday gift from my niece. Never sent me a thing before, but now that I've hit the big six-oh, I guess she expects me to kick off any time now. Probably hoping to get written into the will, the money-grubbing little bitch. Well, I got news for her—that is not going to happen. Anyway, Paul and I are going away for a couple of days, and I said to him, I said, 'Paul, those flowers are nice to look at regardless of who sent them. Why let them wither away in an empty house when they could brighten the lives of others?' So enjoy, darlin'. They're all yours now."

"Thanks, Mrs. Figard," said Ava. "Have fun on your trip. Happy birthday!"

She considered putting the flowers on the dining room table, but that would have meant relocating the everyday centerpiece, and she had no idea where to put it. You couldn't really call Ava's house cluttered, but you might say it was thoroughly decorated. Every table, every counter, every windowsill had been claimed by a knickknack or a vase or a potted plant. Mrs. Figard's flowers would displace something no matter where they ended up.

And then she got her great idea. She was the only person in her family who knew about the flowers, so why not keep it that way? She had a better place in mind for them—the spot where Deej had died. Sometimes when a person got killed in a car accident, their loved ones placed flowers at the accident site. So far, nobody had done that for Deej. Ava knew because she and her friends often walked over to Bugbane Rock to pray and cry and rail at the injustice of it all.

Well, if she was going to do this, she should do it soon, before her family got back. The flowers were really pretty, and once Ava's mom saw them, she would want to keep them.

Ava balked at the thought of going out alone. But today, on this busy Saturday, none of her primary peeps were available. Kylie was visiting her cousins in Raleigh, Kalisha had a volleyball game, Paisley's feet were too swollen to walk anywhere, Charlie was probably babysitting, and as for Blake, Ava was still ticked off at him over their most recent argument, though she couldn't quite remember what they'd argued about.

She stood in the kitchen, staring out the window over the sink. Her backyard abutted Mr. Baldwin's field, which abutted the patch of woods that flowed onto school grounds. Bugbane Rock was less than half a mile from Ava's back porch, a ten-minute walk. Shorter than that if she jogged part of the way. She could be there and back within twenty minutes.

Her eyes roved across the field, all the way to the scribble of woods at the far end. Not a soul was in sight. Anyway, it seemed unlikely that a kidnapper would lurk in such a secluded area, just waiting for a victim to wander by. She was probably safer in the wilds of Pinedale's suburbs than she was on the streets of the town. Yesterday's close call had underscored that.

When she weighed everything out, a quick trip to Bugbane Rock seemed like a low-risk venture on this pleasant Saturday afternoon. Deej would have his flowers! But just in case she was wrong about the kidnapper, she slipped a tube of pepper spray into her pocket.

The sun shone down on her as she set off across Mr. Baldwin's field. She was glad the rain of the past few days had ended—for the time being, anyway. Oops, she'd forgotten to grab her phone, but that was okay. She wouldn't be gone that long. She followed the path etched into the ground by ATV tires, praying Mr. Baldwin wouldn't pop out of his house and scream at her to get off his property. What a jerk that guy was.

Whoa. What was that? Ava came to a halt, using a hand to shade her eyes. There, ten feet in front of her, was a copperhead snake sunning itself on a flat rock.

She considered aborting her mission but in the end decided to press on. It was easy enough to avoid the snake. She would just have to give it wide berth. She veered thirty feet to the right before angling back toward the path. And then, before she even had time to cry out, the earth gave way beneath her and she plummeted forty feet underground.

It was eerie how circumstances had converged to bring her to that moment. The flowers, the Figards' travel plans, her family's absence, the snake. Of course, that was the curse working its magic. If Ava had somehow managed to steer clear of the abandoned well, the curse would have found some other way to make her disappear.

How could she be so stupid? She should have known the curse would have its way.

The next three days passed in a blur of misery. The shaft was so narrow that she was upright the whole time. She suspected her ankle was broken because of how badly it hurt. She was also exhausted, cold, hungry, and thirsty. Luckily, it rained intermittently on Sunday and Monday, so she was able to catch raindrops on her tongue as they dripped down from above. She also wrung rainwater from her jacket sleeves into her mouth. It wasn't much, but it staved off death by dehydration.

She screamed her throat raw, knowing all the while how unlikely it was that anyone would hear her. *Disappear forever*—that was the fate the card had ordained.

And then yesterday morning, while she'd been half dozing with her head lolling forward, she'd heard voices. People were in the field. She screamed, and they heard her, and the fire department came with a long rope and hauled her to safety.

Coincidentally, the people who'd found her—Deej's aunt and grandmother—had been taking flowers to the spot where Deej had died.

Mr. Baldwin was in trouble with the law, since the incident had taken place on his property. The well had been dug decades ago by his grandfather as he prepared to build a homestead on the land he'd recently purchased. But when the well drillers encountered a thick layer of rock that would have been difficult and expensive to drill through, he'd moved the whole operation five hundred feet away, where the ground was more yielding.

The wooden plank that had covered the opening to the abandoned well had long since rotted away. Mr. Baldwin had forgotten the old well even existed, and no one else knew about it. The opening was hidden by the tall weeds and grasses that grew in the field.

Mr. Baldwin would have to pay a hefty fine, and he'd been ordered to fill in the hole at his own expense. Blake had stopped by this morning on his way to school to tell Ava about it. He'd visited her yesterday afternoon, too, and had stayed for more than an hour. They'd both apologized for their recent bickering. Ava was thankful their friendship was back on track.

"Hey, girlfriend. You awake?"

Ava glanced up and saw Maddy standing in the doorway.

"Hey, Mads. Come on in."

Chapter 34

Maddy

Coincidentally (but not really), Ava and Maddy had turned up on the same day.

Physically, Maddy was in better shape than Ava. Although she'd been gone longer, she'd been well fed during her absence. She wasn't dehydrated, and she had no broken bones. She'd been brought to the hospital for overnight observation after suffering a mild concussion.

That car had whizzed around the bend so fast that she hadn't had time to get out of the way. It had screeched to a stop, but not before the front bumper tapped her. The tap knocked her down, and she hit her head on the pavement.

Dizzy and panicked, she'd tried to scuttle away, certain that Tommy was about to burst out of the car with his gun. But the driver had turned out to be someone from the very house Maddy was trying to get to. The lady was an unabashed Karen type, but that was okay. She was actually pretty nice and insisted on driving Maddy to the hospital.

The area where Tommy and the Karen lady lived was halfway between Raleigh and Pinedale, so it was a matter of deciding whether to turn left or right at the highway interchange. Raleigh, being a larger city, probably had better options in terms of medical care, but Maddy had asked to be taken to Pinedale. Home sweet home. During the car ride, the Karen lady dialed nine-one-one to report that her neighbor was a serial killer and to ream out the nine-one-one operator for not nabbing him sooner, even though catching serial killers wasn't that person's job.

Maddy's mom and Ron were at the hospital when Maddy arrived, having been notified by the police—and oh, what a joyous reunion that was. Maddy's mom stayed overnight in her hospital room, though all she did was pace around chewing her fingernails. Maddy couldn't sleep either, convinced that Tommy was on his way to the hospital to finish her off. She knew she was being irrational—things like that happened only in thriller movies—but Ron took her concerns very seriously and stationed himself outside her door like a security guard, despite the fact that he had no weapons except for his bare hands.

Around midnight a police officer came by to tell them that Tommy had been apprehended at a gas station in Virginia and was now in jail. He'd confessed to murdering "a couple of girls," whose bodies he'd buried in his backyard. Excavation would begin the following day.

"Did you get interviewed by the newspaper?" Ava asked Maddy.

Maddy dragged a chair close to Ava's bed and sat down. "Yeah. Dude came by this morning. A couple of the Raleigh papers called, too."

Ava laughed—but it wasn't a happy laugh. "You, me, and Deej—that's a lot of excitement for a town this small."

Maddy's heart did a sorrowful bobble at the

mention of Deej. Last night her mom had told her about the accident, and now every time his name came up, every time Maddy thought of him, she teared up. "I can't believe he's gone," she said, swiping at her eyes with both hands. "I really needed to see him."

"You still can," said Ava. And she repeated what Blake had told her yesterday.

Maddy barely breathed as she listened. "Deej is haunting the high school? That's...that's..." She gave a sob that had a laugh embedded in it. "...it's so Deej!"

Ava grinned, her own eyes shining with tears. "I know. I can't wait to see him."

"Maybe I'll go over there tonight. Well—" Maddy hesitated. "—if I can get somebody to drive me."

Already the agoraphobia had set in, the fear that the second she stepped outside, she would be snatched. As if serial killers were as plentiful as birds and they all had their sights set on her. The hospital counselor who'd met with her this morning said her fears were normal. Maddy was suffering from PTSD, and it would take time to get over it. The counselor recommended that she follow up with a good therapist.

"I hear you're getting discharged soon," said Ava.

"Yeah. I guess my parents are still having lunch with your parents. Once they're done yakking, they're coming to get me."

"Lucky you," said Ava.

"Lucky both of us," Maddy said solemnly. "We could just as easily have ended up like Deej."

Their eyes met in a shared moment of gratitude. They were alive!

Still, things weren't that simple for Maddy, because there were different levels of being alive, just like in those video games Charlie liked to play. It was true that she'd survived the kidnapping, but she felt as if her old life had ended the moment she'd entered Tommy's car. A new era had begun, one that heralded a bolder, more confident Maddy. Never again would she sit back and accept whatever the fates handed her. Whether it was pressure to play a game or to accept a ride from a stranger, she, Maddy, would be the one in charge of deciding. And if her choices offended anybody, too freakin' bad.

Her new life had already delivered an interesting plot twist. Last night, during those long, sleepless hours, her mom had finally come clean about her past. She'd told Maddy about Mr. Trinkley and even, for the first time, about Maddy's father. It turned out she did know who he was—a guy named Shane who'd died before Maddy had been born. Shane had been a deeply flawed person, but he'd also had a sweet side that not many people saw. Laura had loved him since ninth grade, though the two of them hadn't hooked up romantically until shortly before his death. She hadn't found out she was pregnant till after he'd died, and she'd never told anyone who the baby's father was. Now, suddenly, it had become clear to her that Maddy had a right to know her paternal relatives.

Maddy said sure, she would be happy to meet her dad's family. She would let them love her if that was what they wanted, and maybe she would even love them back. But as far as she was concerned, Ron was her true father, Ron's parents were her grandparents, and nothing would ever change that.

Elijah poked his head into Ava's room. "Maddy? Your parents are back. You ready to get out of here?"

Maddy Eppley squared her shoulders and prepared to rejoin the world.

Chapter 35

The *would you rather* twenty-three

Name: Alyssa Aiken
Would-you-rather scenario: Amazing artist / brilliant mathematician
Choice: Amazing artist
Came true? Yes
Follow-up: Alyssa's artistic ability dried up immediately, and she resumed her dream of opening a hair salon.

****

Name: Paisley Boyd
Would-you-rather scenario: Swollen hands / swollen feet
Choice: Swollen feet
Came true? Yes
Follow-up: Paisley's feet quickly shrank back down to their normal size with no residual effects.

****

Name: Jared Crofton
Would-you-rather scenario: Win $1,000 / be honored for doing something heroic
Choice: Win $1,000
Came true? Yes
Follow-up: Jared had already spent the money. Two days after the curse ended, he wrecked his car. The

insurance company sent him a check for repairs, but he had to pay a $1,000 deductible.

****

Name: Maddy Eppley

Would-you-rather scenario: Accidentally kill someone / get kidnapped by a serial killer

Choice: Kidnapped by a serial killer

Came true? Yes

Follow-up: Three days after the curse ended, Maddy escaped from her captor. As of late December, he was lodged in the Wake County jail awaiting trial. Law enforcement officials said they fully expected him to be sentenced to life in prison with no possibility of parole. The bodies of nine young women were found buried in his yard, including his first victim, Rachel, who'd vanished sixteen years earlier.

****

Name: Reina Ichikawa

Would-you-rather scenario: Go bald / grow excessive body hair

Choice: Go bald

Came true? Yes

Follow-up: Reina's hair grew back unusually fast. By late December, it was almost down to her chin.

****

Name: Ben Lawrence

Would-you-rather scenario: Chronic b.o. / breath that smells like rotting garbage

Choice: Garbage breath

Came true? Yes

Follow-up: Ben's breath was back to normal the morning after the curse ended. But he'd purchased so many bottles of minty mouthwash that he now had a ten-year supply.

****

Name: Jonathan Liebfried

Would-you-rather scenario: Go blind / lose ability to speak

Choice: Lose ability to speak

Came true? Yes, though most people didn't notice because Jonathan wasn't much of a talker.

Follow-up: Three days after the curse ended, Jonathan discovered his voice was back when a teacher called on him in class.

****

Name: Zoe Malinowski

Would-you-rather scenario: Roast to death / freeze to death

Choice: Freeze to death

Came true? No

Follow-up: Zoe, who had fled to Miami to avoid her fate, moved back to Pinedale after the curse ended.

****

Name: Brianna McFeaters

Would-you-rather scenario: Bedbug infestation / spider infestation

Choice: Bedbug infestation

Came true? Yes

Follow-up: The bedbug population started to decrease immediately. Within four days, Brianna's house was bug-free.

****

Name: Deej Nolty

Would-you-rather scenario: die of cancer / be killed in a vehicular collision

Choice: Vehicular collision

Came true? Yes

Follow-up: Deej stayed dead but returned as a ghost to haunt the high school.

****

Name: Liam Oswalt

Would-you-rather scenario: Grotesque rash / chronic diarrhea

Choice: Grotesque rash

Came true? Yes

Follow-up: Liam's rash cleared up within a day.

****

Name: Kalisha Parker

Would-you-rather scenario: Fall from a great height / be trapped underwater

Choice: Trapped underwater

Came true? No

Follow-up: Not applicable

****

Name: Blake Pedley

Would-you-rather scenario: Lose cell phone / lose a limb

Choice: Lose cell phone

Came true? Yes

Follow-up: Blake's original phone reappeared moments after the curse ended. The burner phone he'd purchased showed up the following day, so now he had two.

****

Name: Anthony Primavera

Would-you-rather scenario: Stung by a swarm of bees / attacked by wild dogs

Choice: Wild dogs

Came true? No

Follow-up: Not applicable

****

Name: Will Rowland

Would-you-rather scenario: Be decapitated / be poisoned to death

Choice: Decapitated

Came true? No

Follow-up: Not applicable

****

Name: Valentina Sanchez

Would-you-rather scenario: Nothing amazing ever happens / amazing things countered by terrible things

Choice: Amazing things countered by terrible things

Came true? Yes

Follow-up: Val never heard from Finn Rowdy again. When she tried to call him, she found that he'd blocked her number. Subsequent medical tests found no trace of cancer in Val's grandmother.

****

Name: Vishnu Singh

Would-you-rather scenario: Lost in the woods / lost in a high-crime area of a big city

Choice: Lost in the woods

Came true? No

Follow-up: Not applicable

****

Name: Lonnie Turko

Would-you-rather scenario: Lose your mother / lose your father

Choice: Lose your mother

Came true? Almost. Mrs. Turko narrowly avoided a fatal car accident the night the curse ended.

Follow-up: Lonnie reported that her mother was now an ultra-cautious driver.

****

Name: Charlie Washington

Would-you-rather scenario: Get the romantic partner of your dreams / land the perfect job

Choice: Land the perfect job

Came true? Yes

Follow-up: Charlie received a letter from V-Play cancelling his game-testing contract. The company said they initially hadn't realized he was only sixteen. According to company policy, no one under eighteen could be a V-Play game tester.

****

Name: Kylie Wentworth

Would-you-rather scenario: Lose your best friend / lose all your friends except your best friend

Choice: Lose your best friend

Came true? Yes

Follow up: Kalisha made up with Kylie, saying she couldn't remember what she'd been mad about.

****

Name: Ava Wilkinson

Would-you-rather scenario: You disappear forever / person you love most disappears forever

Choice: You disappear forever

Came true? Yes

Follow-up: Ava was rescued from an abandoned well three days after the curse ended.

****

Name: DeShawn Yancy

Would-you-rather scenario: Be shocked every time you touch metal / be pooped on by birds every time you go outside

Choice: Pooped on by birds

Came true? Yes

Follow-up: The day after the curse ended, Pinedale's birds stopped pooping on DeShawn. Unfortunately, he'd already cut off his beautiful dreadlocks because he couldn't get all the bird poop out of them.

****

Name: Natalie Yoon

Would-you-rather scenario: Be able to read incredibly fast / be able to type incredibly fast

Choice: Read incredibly fast

Came true? No

Follow-up: Not applicable

****

Addendum: Officer Murphy of the Pinedale Police Department awoke from his coma two days after the curse ended and returned to work a few days later.

Chapter 36

Blake

Feeble January sunlight glimmered beyond Blake's bedroom window as he sat at his desk, studying the spreadsheet on his computer screen. The spreadsheet stared back impassively. It contained the names of everyone in the *would you rather* group, along with the details of each person's curse. After Mr. Trinkley agreed to end the curse, Ava had let a month go by to see how everything played out. Then she'd plugged in the follow-up data and sent the finalized spreadsheet to the surviving members of the group.

No one could accuse Ava of being half-assed. She threw her full ass into everything she did.

Blake was sure some of the recipients would delete the spreadsheet without looking at it, because all they wanted to do was forget. Whereas he felt compelled to remember. Perusing the entries gave him closure. It was like reading twenty-three little stories, each with a beginning, a middle, and an end.

Would you rather had been like a dating app, he thought, except instead of bringing lovers together, it had matched victims with their fates—and, in a few cases, winners with their prizes. Blake hadn't fared as badly as some, but he was still mighty glad the curse had ended.

Of course, you couldn't really say the story had ended with a happily ever after. People had been to hell and back, and some now suffered from PTSD. Blake himself had developed a neuroticism that compelled him to pat his pockets every few minutes to confirm the whereabouts of his phone. Valentina still moped around, mourning the loss of her celebrity admirer. DeShawn carried an umbrella every time he went outside. Even the people whose curses hadn't been activated were on edge, half-expecting their chosen fate to pounce on them out of the blue, like a stealthy cougar.

Overshadowing all that anxiety was the school's collective grief over Deej. Most people believed he was gone for good and still struggled to accept his death.

Blake, Ava, and Charlie were among the lucky few who knew Deej was still around. They often sneaked into the school after hours to hang out with him. The Alphabet Quartet, back together again. It wasn't the same as before, but at least it was something. The four of them bantered, reminisced, shared confidences, and sometimes played board games. Deej had been pleasantly surprised to find that he could move objects. Blake wondered if that made him a poltergeist.

Deej didn't abuse his ghostly powers, but he sometimes used them in slightly impish ways. One night Ava had complained to the group about how Mr. Zwick always picked on her. The next day in physics class, Mr. Zwick's dry erase marker kept falling off the little ledge at the bottom of the whiteboard. No sooner would he put it back than it would drop to the floor again. Blake had to fight to keep a straight face, certain that Deej was behind the mischief.

The next time they visited Deej, Charlie laughed and said, "What you did to Zwick was epic, man. But I have an even better idea for next time."

Deej shook his head. "Not gonna be a next time, bro. I'm done with teacher pranks."

Blake understood where he was coming from. Twenty years ago, teacher-pranking had led to Mr. Trinkley's death. How could Charlie even suggest that they continue to torment Mr. Zwick? Hadn't he learned anything from their experience?

Blake found it curious, though, that Deej had reached the same conclusion. Deej, who in life had channeled his chronic anger into jokes and pranks, seemed mellow and benevolent in death. Happy, even. Blake thought he knew why.

Sometimes when he and his friends arrived at the school, they would find Maddy already there with Deej. The two of them would get a startled look, like burglars interrupted by a police raid. Something was going on between them, some weird situationship that they were keeping on the down low.

The subtle looks they gave each other reminded Blake of those movies about the teenage girl and the sparkly vampire dude. Of course, that was a different situation altogether. First of all, both the girl and the vampire had actual solid bodies. Second, that story was Hollywood fiction, whereas the thing between Deej and Maddy was real. Was a romantic relationship between a ghost and a living girl possible? The idea was weird.

Of course, Blake could accept weirdness because he'd seen so much of it over the past four months. What could be weirder than a twenty-three-pronged curse, one that let you choose your own destiny? Nowadays he spent a lot of time thinking back on the whole thing. Trying to find the positives in what had been a decidedly negative experience.

Deej's dad had straightened himself out—that was one good thing that had come out of it. No more drinking, no more loose women, and he worked hard at his job. He even had a respectable new girlfriend—the owner of a local bookstore.

Ava and Maddy had become teen activists. Ava's platform was abandoned wells, and she'd gotten county officials to approve a tax rebate for rural residents who filled in old wells on their properties. Meanwhile, Maddy had been visiting schools throughout the county to talk about her experience and give tips on how to escape from a kidnapper.

Blake was proud of his friends. Who knew? Maybe lives would be saved because of their efforts.

He gave a start as somebody pounded on his bedroom door. It had to be Max, his brother. Nobody else abused his door like that.

"Hey, Blako-flako, the bird poop kid is here."

"Be down in a minute," called Blake. He took a last look at the spreadsheet before closing it out.

He and DeShawn were going to collect Charlie and then meet some other guys at the high school to shoot hoops. DeShawn had gone on his first date with Jade Zimmer last night, and Blake couldn't wait to hear about it. He'd suspected for a while that DeShawn liked Jade. The longing glances he gave her when he thought no one was watching had made it obvious. Blake had been thrown off when Jade went to the Christmas dance with Drew Sanderson and DeShawn went with Amber Blackburn. But neither of those pairings had led anywhere, and now DeShawn and Jade had zeroed in on each other. Blake wished them well. He thought they were perfect together.

For the dozenth time since he'd sat down at his computer, his gaze drifted to the right side of the desk, where his cell phone sat, waiting to be of service. He laid a hand on it, making sure it was as solid as it looked. Then he turned back to his computer and created a folder called "Physics Class." He renamed Ava's spreadsheet "Homework" and dragged it into the new folder. There. The spreadsheet was now hidden away, unlikely to be opened by nosy little brothers or curious moms. He intended to look at it now and then to rehash the lessons he'd learned from *would you rather*. They were important lessons, and he never wanted to forget.

Live each day to the fullest, because you never know when it might be your last.

Treat others the way you want to be treated.

Never piss off a ghost.

And maybe the most valuable lesson of all:

Don't tempt fate.

A word about the author...

Kimberly Baer wrote her first story at age six. It was about a baby chick that hatched out of a little girl's Easter egg after somehow surviving the hard-boiling process. Nowadays she writes in a variety of genres, including young adult, middle-grade, and adult romantic suspense. She lives in Virginia, where she likes to go power-walking on days when it's not too hot, too cold, too rainy, too snowy, or too windy. On indoor days, you might find her hard at work on her next novel or binge-watching old episodes of Survivor, her favorite guilty pleasure.

You can call her Kim; all her friends do. Visit her at www.kimberlybaer.com.